The Promise

and other stories

Stories to make you think, shiver and smile

National Short Story Week Young Writers

Published by Stories Unlimited C.I.C.
20-22 Wenlock Road, London N1 7GU
www.nationalshortstoryweek.org.uk

ISBN: 1519268971
ISBN-13: 978-1519268976

All of the royalties from sales of this anthology will go to Teenage Cancer Trust to support them in their work.

INTRODUCTION

This anthology contains the twenty-one short-listed stories from the National Short Story Week Young Writer 2015 competition, as well as some of the best stories from our previous competitions.

Over the past five years, more than five hundred schools have taken part in the National Short Story Week Young Writer Competition, with many thousands of school children writing short stories.

Each year, pupils in years 7 and 8 write a short story based on a title which we provide. And each year, we are struck by the inventiveness with which the children interpret the title they are given. This year was no exception, with an impressive range of stories, to make you think, shiver and smile.

Our young writers are not afraid to address difficult subjects and ideas, and their stories show a remarkable level of maturity of thought and expression.

All of the proceeds from this anthology will be donated to Teenage Cancer Trust. We couldn't think of a better way to celebrate the success of our young writers than to have their work available in print, and for that work to help young people and their families who are going through a challenging time in their lives. The writers can take pride in knowing that their stories will make a difference to other young people just like them.

The first story in the book is the overall winning story, by our National Short Story Week Young Writer. The remaining stories do not appear in a ranked order; they are published in the order which we think best reflects the variety of themes and styles found in the short-listed entries. A full list of the writers and their achievements can be found at the end of this book.

We are delighted to share their stories with you.

Ian Skillicorn
Director, National Short Story Week

ONE

I stand over him, knife poised to kill. Clenching my weapon in one hand, I pin him down on the ground with the other, my eyes fixated on his once handsome face. A single bead of sweat runs down his forehead, glistening in the flickering candle light. His lips are paralysed in a quivering circle; his eyes resemble those of a terror-stricken animal, bloodshot and frantic as they scan the room for a method of escape.

Inside my head I laugh bitterly. Doesn't Philip know I already drugged the guards outside, so no one will hear his screams? He is my prisoner; I will not allow him to escape the fate he unknowingly declared for himself when he cut a scar in my heart so deep it would never heal.

It's taken me two years to hunt him down. Two years of sleeping rough, surviving on little or nothing, with no one to turn to for aid. The only thing that has kept me alive was the eternal thirst for revenge that has numbed my heart to stone and transformed me into something inhumane.

'Elizabeth,' he rasps, pleadingly. 'Please. *Please*, Bess.'

Anger surges like fire through my body at the sound of my old pet name, inflaming my heart and flowing down to my fingertips. I clasp the knife harder, and the little colour left in Philip's face disappears. Every nerve in my body explodes in fury and adrenaline; vengeance is so unbearably close.

Then I catch a glimpse of my reflection in the crude blade of the knife. A girl, with dark hair, hacked away at neck-length, framing her hollow face so covered in filth I hardly recognise her, stares back. I immediately think of my mother, and pain stabs into my heart as I am dragged back to the day of her murder.

He came in the dead of the night.

I awoke from my sleep at the piercing sound of my mother's scream. I hadn't ever experienced true fear before in my life, I'd never had a reason to be afraid, but hearing her voice suddenly struck pure terror into my heart. At first I lay, petrified, desperately trying to comprehend what was happening. Thieves were certainly not uncommon in our village, but I knew we possessed nothing truly worth stealing.

Suddenly, I came to my senses and immediately flung myself out of my bed, rushing to my mother's room. I had to find her.

But the screaming had stopped. I was too late.

He crouched beside her limp body, clenching a knife streaked with blood. My mother's blood.

In his other hand was a small glistening ring. I took a sharp breath inwards as I recognised the precious object; it belonged to my father, a victim of the plague that struck many years ago. He gave my mother the ring on his deathbed. It had been the only thing we had left to remind us of him after he disappeared from our lives forever, the only true treasure we would ever possess. Of course my mother would have put up a fight.

Now this man had murdered her for it.

I could not scream or cry. All emotions seemed to have left my body completely, replacing them with a monotonous pit of emptiness. I stared at him, the man who had just annihilated everything I loved and cared for in a heartbeat.

The killer's face was concealed by a piece of cloth, tied around his head, revealing only his eyes. He gazed back at me, clearly determining how much of a threat I posed to him. A girl of my age was no match for a man with a knife, but if I screamed for help now, surely someone would hear me.

A few agonising seconds passed. His only way out was through the doorway in which I now stood. My mind screamed for me to step away, allow him to escape or I would surely end up with the same fate as my mother. But suddenly a desperate urge to seek revenge took a hold of my mind, pumping adrenaline into my blood and filling me with a fury I'd never before experienced. I would make him pay.

I lunged. Immediately, he made for the door, but my hands closed around the cloth hiding his face.

My eyes widened in dismay, for the face beneath the cloth was Philip's, my childhood sweetheart. Philip, the boy who worked at the baker's down the street, who had sworn to love me for all eternity, who had even spoken of us marrying when we became old enough. Philip, who had just murdered my mother and stolen my most prized possession. He was my most trusted companion; I had told him of the ring many years ago and now his greed had got the better of him.

'Philip?' I whispered in horrified disbelief.

'Bess. I …' There was regret in Philip's voice but clearly he had no words to justify what he had done. He hesitated, but then backed out of the door as I sunk to my knees beside my mother's body.

I lost all track of time, though it took a while for the heartbreak to sink in. I had nothing, no one, nowhere to go to. He'd taken everything from me.

And then the anger came, beginning as a tiny spark, but gradually growing to a roaring fire. Only one thing would extinguish it.

'Mother,' I whispered into the night air. 'I will avenge you. I promise.'

'Bess, please don't.' Philip's gutless pleading strains me back into reality. 'I'll give you anything.'

'I want my mother back!' My voice breaks as tears suddenly come cascading down my cheeks. My hatred and rage vanishes, replaced only with grief and longing to be with my mother.

Finally I accept the truth. Murdering Philip won't bring her back. Taking his life will only make me the same person he is.

I cannot keep my promise.

Amber Lahdelma
Tunbridge Wells Girls' Grammar School
National Short Story Week Young Writer 2015

TWO

The Stone had always been there. Even in myths and legends, the Stone and the Promise had always been mentioned. It had always been that way.

I could see the Stone from my bedroom window, the top floor of the tallest tower. It was a large stone slab in the hillside with the Promise inscribed upon it. The Stone scared me slightly – mainly because it was my job to continue the Promise as queen of this country. My one job: do not break the Promise. When I was eighteen I was crowned – both my parents died when I was six (I can barely remember them) so on that day, though surrounded by my many hundreds of subjects, I had never felt more alone. Now, I was twenty; in three months' time, when I became twenty-one, my court would finally take me up to the hill to see the Promise. Until then I could only guess.

There was a gentle tap on my door, as if the person on the other side was afraid of what was inside. They probably were.

'Your Majesty?' I didn't know that voice – a boy's, about the same age as me I thought, though I couldn't say until I saw him. 'Um … I have a message for you …' This was something I could hazard a guess on: *the court is waiting for you.*

I opened the door with a frustrated sigh.

'Let me guess,' I said. 'The court is wai-' my voice caught in my throat when I saw him. Blond hair, blue eyes – the opposite to me. He wasn't handsome, but he had a spark of adventure in his eyes. I had a fleeting image of the two of us climbing trees and river walking in the forest at the base of the hill.

'Um … your Majesty? I'm your new manservant, my name's Luke –'

'Call me Jane,' I heard myself say. 'I was just looking at the hill – well, the Stone – you know – the Promise, I mean – and I was thinking, sun's bright today isn't it? But not too bright – well, yes it is bright – but cold as well – oh God, I'm talking about the *weather* …' Luke smiled and I blushed, kicking myself for jabbering on like that.

'It is bright, and cold, but thankfully no wind. Good day for tree climbing.'

'You climb trees?'

We went downstairs, into the grounds to the forest. I suppose you could say I had the best time of my life there, climbing to the top of the forest's highest trees, picking and eating the different fruits under the emerald canopy. It was so nice to have a real friend, not one of those stuck-up duchesses who wants a boyfriend, or a pretentious count that spends his time organizing his week.

Luke was a kind, funny and awkward baker's son who a queen shouldn't spend time with. We were out for hours, and it never occurred once to either of us that I was supposed to go to court to discuss the well-being of my subjects. I know now that was the worst decision I could have ever made.

It started the day after we had gone out – there was panic in the city (called Capitalia) because no one was getting any bread. As queen, it was my duty to go and see what the matter was. Upon arriving at the bakery, my guards had to push through the crowds to get to the door. A woman – the baker's wife – was clutching the body of a boy to her chest and sobbing. The baker was sitting with his arms around her, tears falling silently. Neither looked up when I entered. I left my guards standing at the doorway and approached the couple. She looked up at me, her wide eyes red and puffy.

'Is that your son?' I asked. She didn't answer but the tears falling faster at my words told me I was right. 'May I see him?' The woman moved her arm enough to let me see the boy. I gasped. I could recognise those stunningly blue eyes staring, unseeing, anywhere.

Luke was dead.

A week later there was an earthquake, killing hundreds and turning the once beautiful city to rubble. The palace lost the servants' quarters. I don't know how many servants died. There was billions of pounds of damage done.

Exactly one month on, I went to a parliament, in a city called Albove, to discuss the problem of drought. An hour into the meeting, everyone had to be evacuated because of a flood. Only the rich citizens got away: most of the poor drowned. On the train back home, the hot discussion was why the flood had happened. There had been no rain for months, no river nearby and the sea was miles away – besides, none of the areas in between the ocean and Albove had been affected.

It was a lightning storm next. Three weeks from my

birthday, a bolt of sharp lightning hit Capitalia in the most important places – the meeting hall, the food shops, the army centre – before the storm gathered itself and destroyed my tower. Then it left as quickly as it had come.

Finally, after years of waiting, my birthday came. There was a parade through what used to be a shining beacon of a city, but now all of Capitalia had bigger problems. It was a hot day, so on the walk up to the Stone I was sweating like a sinner in church, but it finally appeared on the horizon. The court stopped, to let me walk up alone, for only the reigning queen was to see the Promise.

I squinted at the weathered rock trying to make out the Latin inscription. I read it and translated it. Then my heart went cold.

nunquam aliquem in iudicio.
Never put anyone before the court.

The Promise was broken.

Julia Harmon
The King's School in Macclesfield

THREE

I pushed the green button and there it was. Ten minutes earlier and I had stepped wearily into my flat at the end of another humdrum day. I had been on autopilot. Kick off shoes. Pour a cold beer. Search for remote control. Switch on television. Now my senses were alive. Now nothing would ever be the same.

There it was. The face I knew so well, staring out of the screen at me. But it was puckered and gaunt, nothing like I remembered it. This face was weathered and lined, turned nut-brown by a harsh sun literally a world away from the insipid sun in the Manchester suburb where we had grown up together. The colour of his face radiated warmth, but I was shocked to see that the eyes were cold. Gone the mischievous sparkle that I could conjure up in my mind's eye now as I stared at Tom, my boyhood friend, on the screen. Gone the twinkle that had always made me smile as we set off on another childish adventure. The eyes that looked back at me now did not dance with life; they were dull, expressionless, soulless. As I dragged my gaze from those appalling eyes, the rest of the scene came into focus – behind the figure a flag I recognised: Syria, a second flag with writing on it: Arabic. In a flash my thoughts focused themselves too – he was in trouble and someone had to help him. I had to.

As I hastily switched off the television, my senses were assaulted again, this time by the metallic tang of blood in my mouth. How vivid the memory triggered by this astringent taste! I was transported back thirty years to an unexpectedly sunny day in Moss Side. We were barely teenagers, but I remembered it like it was yesterday. I had fallen foul of a tough gang of yobs on our run-down housing estate, foolishly straying onto their 'turf' and suffering a beating that broke my nose, split my lip and left me dazed. Disturbed, the yobs had scattered, vowing to come back and finish the job. As I lay on the hard ground, I looked up to see – Tom. My saviour. It was at that moment, as we stared at one another, that we became blood brothers. Not like in some Hollywood movie where drops of blood are mingled to seal a relationship forever. We did not need such melodrama to know that ours was now an unbreakable friendship, and we made an unspoken but unbreakable promise – always to be there for one another. Here was a chance to repay my debt. If he needed me, I would be there. It was clear in my mind. I would go.

Unable to be dissuaded, I travelled with a charity delivering aid to Syria. I had done my research, knew where Tom had been based as a journalist and where the terrorists operated in this area. The charity didn't take me far enough, so I stowed away in the engine compartment of a train travelling deep into the Syrian countryside. I was alone and scared, but I was fuelled by a determination to find my friend and fulfil a promise made decades ago on the other side of the world. I would die in the attempt if I had to.

I sat in the cramped and sweltering engine compartment for what felt like days. I had no way of gauging the true passage of time, as my chamber was sealed from the outside world. All I saw was the glow of the engine, which was so stiflingly hot that I felt sure I would suffocate. All I heard was the train juddering along the rugged track, so jarring that several times I thought we were derailing and had to hold back the scream that threatened to erupt from me. All I felt was panic. The petrol fumes filled my lungs with every breath and I longed to cough, but I could not make so much as a squeak for fear of being heard by the driver who was only two metres away in the next compartment. Terror. Horror. Dread. Agony. Would I survive? Would I be caught? Would I find him? A mind full of questions and not one answer. The walls began to close in on me.

As the train finally shuddered to a halt I curled myself tightly into a ball. I heard passengers, luggage and animals being unloaded. After about an hour the hubbub finally died down and I allowed my aching limbs to stretch a little. The pain in my body was subsiding, but the agony of fear was as acute as ever. When I could bear the claustrophobic heat of my prison no longer. I pushed the door open a fraction. The driver had gone. I filled my lungs with the clean, clear air and felt the cold muzzle of a rifle on my temple.

Twenty of us. Packed into a tiny cell. Some were moaning, some wailing, others completely silent, but all were desperate, all terrified. I scanned the hopeless faces looking for Tom, but he wasn't there. I looked down in horror at my orange jumpsuit. It was not in a Hollywood movie that I had seen these jumpsuits before, but in countless news bulletins over the past year as innocent victims were brutally beheaded by a merciless group of terrorists. I wept silently as we prisoners were shackled and led out into the searing sunshine. When I looked up from my shuffling feet, a pair of cold, soulless eyes met mine and smiled. Brandishing a machete the executioner was waiting for me with a look of anticipation on his face, a face that was so familiar. I had found Tom. Here was my childhood friend, my blood brother, my killer. I knew then that I had been forsaken. I knelt and waited for the blow; had the promise led me to my death?

Joe Wald
Dulwich Prep London

FOUR

'My son, Akimbo, are you ok?' He lay with his head resting back on the white clay, his slow steady breathing, rasping and hissing like a rattlesnake. I could tell he was hungry, begging God for a little more food, something to stop the rumble of his bloated belly. He wished for the food we did not have. Tearfully, I carried him back into the mud hut. 'Akimbo, I promise that by tomorrow I will have food and water to feed us both. Understood?' He nodded weakly as I placed his skeletal body down like a priceless artefact. I waited in the room and watched his chest rise and fall until he slowly drifted off to sleep. The drought had dried up all of our land, cracked our soil and defied any growing blade of green. It had come at a heavy cost.

I remembered what it was like four years ago, when life was good. We had a little blue and white house that Akimbo and I had once painted one afternoon. We lived happily together at the end of the village and luckily it was the only house near to the jungle so we got some privacy, unlike most of the others. Akimbo would play with his friends and eat the delicious fruits we had bought at the market or grown on our trees. I would sit on a bench with his mother, Chiamaka, and watch the wild dogs and birds go about on their daily routine. I loved spending time imagining what the future would be like, if we would have a servant of our own and endless amounts of food or if we would just remain as we were. Either way I would be just as happy. Life drifted on until sadly my wife became sick. She was getting thinner and thinner every day. Soon she was unable to speak or eat. People are like flowers: beautiful until they are unfed; then they begin to fall apart.

They said it was the water that did it. She became sick. Her skin turned yellow and seemed to cling to her every bone. She barely had strength to stroke her son's hair as he lay next to her. She held her smile in her eyes until the heavens took her from our lives, leaving an empty space.

That was when everything fell apart. I was too sad and heavy to go out to work. The local children chanted and laughed at Akimbo for not having a mother. When I finally recovered I had no money, no jobs, no friends and, most of all, no respect. We had to move into a small crumbling hut that seemed to face away from the village with its shame.

People had heard of our fate, yet it was the wrong sort of people who took an interest in our lives. Three days after moving into the mud hut I was introduced into the biggest mistake of my life. Poaching.

The early morning sun was warm, heating up the clay soil beneath my feet. The warmth of it crept into my body, however I knew that later the ground would fry your feet like eggs in a pan. As our food was still scarce, I decided to save the last grubby bread crust for Akimbo. Reaching for my rifle I examined it to make use of time. Its handle was made out of a honey-coloured wood probably taken from one of the forest trees. It was beautiful, the way it was varnished, the way it was carved. I loved and cherished every splinter. The barrel was a different matter. It was covered in dents, beginning to rust and was made of an ugly matte grey metal forged in a black market of some sort. The gun was a mystery to me – how at one end it was warm and beautiful then at the other end it was a cold killing machine. After staring at it for a few more minutes I realised it was warm and the animals were probably out of their hidings.

Once I had followed the secret route I knew that led to an area safe from the poaching rangers, I started my search.

The sun was setting as I began to give up. Nothing had been strolling around in the fields, in the bushes, not even in the sky. I had failed my son and we would have no food for another night and tonight might be Akimbo's last. Suddenly, I heard a slight thump that was slowly getting louder and louder. I crept into a ditch. Surrounded by nettles and vines, I raised my rifle. Slowly yet gracefully I watched an old enormous elephant stumble into the open field leaving her only protection, the wilderness. One elephant's tusk was worth at least six million shillings; I stopped and imagined the riches that we would have, food for a lifetime, a big house and respect. Snapping back into the real world I raised my rifle and aimed, fingers trembling. Looking through the scope I realised how beautiful this creature was, its grey, leathery skin looked thick enough to be on a king's throne and its eyes were like nuggets of amber glowing with light. I could tell that it was full of wisdom and was one of the leaders in the jungle.

Crack!

This was the noise I heard before the elephant slumped towards the ground like a rag doll as its legs crumpled under its weight. The sight of crimson blood trickling down and poisoning its amber eyes was sickening. My mission was accomplished, I stumbled, my stomach heaving, my eyes could not move from this great majestic beast that lay in a vast heap on the dirt track. I realised what I had done was repulsive.

Had keeping my promise been worth this life?

Sam Cohen
Dulwich Prep London

FIVE

Elliot Lewis Trotter was a very well respected and well thought of resident of Omeath, a small seaside village in southern Ireland. Elliot lived a modest life in his little cottage on the edge of the sand, by the sea. He had always lived alone, as he was quite a difficult pig to live with. However, Elliot had a dark, guilty secret. Elliot was a pig, a pig that liked bacon.

It was a frosty Saturday morning and Elliot had just finished his sumptuous breakfast consisting of two eggs, cooked tomatoes, four rashers of bacon, mushrooms and numerous slices of thick, brown bread. But due to his large breakfast Elliot was now out of bacon, so he went to the village market to get some.

Immediately, when Elliot stepped out of his cottage the frosty November air hit him. He grumbled angrily under his breath, this air couldn't be good for him, a senior citizen and all! Yet somehow Eva, Elliot's next door neighbour, heard him (being a rabbit she had extraordinary hearing).

'What are you moaning about?' she demanded. 'It's a

lovely bright morning.'

Elliot just scowled at Eva as he was in a bad enough mood without her irritating him. Just as Elliot was edging away from Eva, Fifi, Eva's sister who lived with her, appeared out of their bungalow.

'Good morning Elliot,' she said. 'Are you going to the market?' Elliot did a silent scream of panic, as the last thing he needed was Eva and Fifi watching his every move, their plucked eyebrows raised (Eva's eyebrows were plucked just a little too severely!) when he was trying to buy bacon!

'Yes,' Elliot finally said reluctantly.

The three of them marched, well, Elliot waddled, up the steep lane to the village square where the market was held every Saturday. Eventually Eva and Fifi left Elliot and wandered off to look at the flowers.

'Finally,' Elliot sighed in relief, 'they're off my back.' Checking his surroundings – left, right, in front, behind, like a panicked meerkat – Elliot decided the coast was clear and headed off to the darkest corner of the square.

A greasy butcher ran the bacon stall, and as Elliot hurried up to him a big, toothless grin appeared on his sly face.

''Ello there! Come to buy sommor bacon?!' he asked, screeching with laughter. Suddenly, filled with guilt and unable to reply, Elliot took the bacon and practically threw the money at the slimy butcher and ran back to his cottage without waiting for Eva and Fifi!

Once back in the safety of his cottage, he retreated to his bedroom for a lie down. Elliot started to think about what he had done, how he had become addicted to bacon, and whether it was too late to turn back to his old, godly ways ...

Elliot found himself walking down a long dirt path, which seemed to be leading nowhere. A thick fog surrounded him, so he could barely see five feet ahead. Lost in his thoughts, Elliot kept walking and walking, completely unaware of any time passing. He noticed now that the fog had all but cleared and that in the distance there was a bright, flickering light. Elliot was thinking about whether or not he would enter the Kingdom of Heaven if he continued to eat bacon; he knew, deep down that he wouldn't. He had a huge choice to make: either eat bacon, and not enter the Kingdom of Heaven, or give up bacon and confess to the priest. But if he confessed to the priest, what would the priest's reaction be? What if he told the whole village that Elliot was a cannib... – Elliot couldn't even say the word.

While Elliot had been walking, he hadn't realised that the light was no longer in the distance; before him was a huge, mahogany table surrounded by flickering candles and covered in hundreds of silver salvers. The mouth-watering smell of food was tickling Elliot's nostrils and he couldn't resist pulling out a red, velvet chair. But just as he was about to sit down he heard a door slam. He spun round and there was Father Twit, a village priest, watching him. He was a wise owl who understood the meaning of life, death, past, present, future and all eternity.

'Elliot,' he said, his voice grave, 'do you realise where you are?'

Elliot looked around and saw that he was no longer on a dirt path but was in a grand room with golden walls, high ceilings and a shiny wooden floor. He shook his head.

'I thought not. You are halfway between Heaven and Hell, and you have a choice, you can either eat the food in front of you or choose not to. It's your decision,' he turned to leave, 'make the right one.'

Elliot was left alone to gather his thoughts. He should

go, he decided. But the smell coming from that food was mouth-watering and he simply couldn't bring himself to leave without having a peek at what was underneath the silver salvers.

Elliot had barely touched the lid when suddenly all of the covers lifted off the food and disappeared into thin air. The plates were stacked high with the finest meats Elliot had ever seen and the greedy pig trait inside Elliot completely took over as he plonked his fat bottom on the red velvet chair and tucked in. The first thing he went for was honey-roasted bacon. Slowly, Elliot lifted his fork closer to his quavering lips and he was about to take his first bite.

'Aahhh!' Elliot screamed. The platter stacked high with bacon had turned into the head of Elliot's cousin Hetty! All of the platters of fine meats had turned into the heads of Elliot's relatives, all staring up at him, their eyes wide.

Elliot woke up panting and sweating. 'I'm going to the church to confess. I'm becoming a vegan!'

Tara Lewis
New Hall School, Chelmsford

SIX

It had been three hundred years. Three hundred years since humanity teetered on the cusp of extinction. Three hundred years since the technology to capture emotions crashed to earth, leaving a blaze of hope behind it. Three hundred years since the Promise.

And at the end of these three hundred years, in the topmost room of a tower of identical units, a boy was staring out of the window at the bustling city below. He was lucky to be here, above the clamour of the city – for even the gaseous guilt released into the dome's artificial atmosphere couldn't quite keep the population of this dome from littering a little. Today, on the three-hundredth anniversary of the Promise's landing, he was one of the elite few fortunate enough to see it.

Harold Blueman, twelve years and ten months old, slammed his hand down on the alarm sensor. The blaring sound shut off at once, to be replaced with the exasperated calls of his parents. Beginning to get ready as slowly as possible, Harold felt a surge of irritability at the fact that his parents even assumed he wanted to go and visit some dusty old exhibit at this time in the morning. He had things to do, video games to play. The Promise didn't interest him. After all, it just served as a power source, nothing more, nothing less. Boring.

'Harold!' called one of his parents from downstairs. 'Harold, come down here at once! We're going to be late!'

Shuffling down the sleek silver staircase, Harold arrived in the kitchen wearing what was no doubt an intensely sullen expression. The kitchen itself looked identical to every other kitchen in this sector, bar the posters and embarrassing childhood photographs on the walls. Harold's father stood next to the door, unusually stern-looking. His mother stood near the counter, close to the yellow pot in which she kept their regulation serotonin sachets. The little yellow packets supposed to 'dispel negative emotion and aid productivity' vanished from their pot every so often. Quite frequently, actually. She gave him a 'look' and pushed the door open, pressing three small, white nutrition cubes into his hand. Hurriedly eating them (they were chalky and tasteless) Harold stepped out of the door of the unit and into the lift, grudgingly accepting his fate.

They arrived an hour later, at a blocky, sterilised building. The museum, which displayed a shiny white sign reading 'Exhibition of Electronics' wouldn't have looked too bad were it not for the steady stream of old, smartly-dressed, altogether boring-looking people ambling through the doors. Harold considered protesting, but his father pulled him in before he could do anything. The walls, of course, were daffodil yellow, and in a corner, where the old people had clustered, stood a member of staff; a woman in a pinstriped suit, with a name-tag that read 'Angela'.

Once everyone had gathered, Angela, produced a hand-held holo-clipboard, and went around the group collecting tickets and ticking off names. Once everyone had been registered, Angela stepped forward.

'Hello,' she said to the group at large. 'My name is Angela, and I will be your guide for today. All of you have been given a fascinating opportunity today, to see a piece of our culture that has been central to the history of the world for the last …'

Harold began to tune out Angela's words, instead choosing to imagine the exciting things his friends could be doing just then. Why on earth was he was stuck in this infernal museum, watching a group of old people gawk over a shiny light in a tin? '… so, without further ado, follow me, and I'll take you there!'

Harold rushed after his parents. He could have run for it, but he had no money and no idea where to go. Better to just get it over with, he decided. The small door Angela had led them through, led into a maze of corridors, wires snaking along the walls. Eventually, they emerged into a room lit so blindingly everyone covered their eyes. Huge cables stretched from the floor to the ceiling, looking almost alive as they twisted and jolted. And in the centre, a round glass container almost seemed to float in mid-air, juddering with electricity, a thousand wires jammed into the top and bottom, and inside the container was a spinning ball of golden light. It pulsed frantically, almost like a heartbeat. Angela was talking again, but nobody seemed to have noticed. They were all staring, open mouthed, at the source of the dome's power.

Angela, trying not to break the silence, muttered something about being able to come closer. The wave of people moved forward, encircling the Promise, whispering and peering in at the tiny light that generated the world's electricity.

Harold took a step closer, strangely reverent. Carefully, he placed a hand on the glass, the light pulsing with panic, until with a crash, the glass shattered.

The Promise, after flying from its cage, let out a panicked buzz. It zoomed around the room, and as the vestiges of travelling power ran out, the room went dark. Angela reached for it, and pulled her hand away hurriedly, raw and blistered. The Promise dashed out of the door, and without stopping to think, Harold dashed after it. It led him outside, out onto the pavement, over fences, under bridges, a twisted race. Eventually, it stopped, blinking and bobbing up and down excitedly. He stepped closer to it. It had chosen the highest hill in the dome, a place Harold had never been before, but at once he understood why. The stars could be seen from here, pinpricks of gold impossibly far away. All the Promise wanted was to go home. It floated towards him, and he understood he had a choice. He could awaken his city, or let the Promise go. It settled in the palm of his hand, and they stood, beneath the stars, the Promise and its Breaker, forever intertwined.

Julia Trier
The King's School in Macclesfield

SEVEN

It's not as bad as people make out, I mean yes, it is awful, but you get used to it after a while. However that doesn't excuse what she did!

They say everyone deserves a second chance, but I am living … make that dead … proof, that some people don't! Why did she do it? What did I ever do to her?

It's not just being alive that I miss, it's my family too! I really do miss them more than anything else!

I still remember that day, that cool autumn day, where the orange leaves blew around in the breeze as Alice and I walked down to the pier. Alice and I were best friends, always spending time together. I really thought she was a good person, but I was misled by her angelic smile.

As Alice and I reached the end of the old wooden pier, Oliver, my little eight-year-old brother, jumped out from behind the huge, blue rubbish bin.

'What are you doing here? Does Mum even know where you are?' I shouted furiously.

'But it's boring at home and, no, Mum doesn't know!' he replied nervously.

'I am sorry for shouting but you shouldn't be here, however seeing as home is at least a good half hour away you may as well stay!'

The three of us walked closer and closer to the water's edge, right next to where the violent waves were crashing against the pier.

Out of nowhere, a monster wave gushed over where we were standing, whipping Alice and Oliver out to sea. I tried to grab them but the force of the water was too strong. I didn't have enough time to save both of them. I had to make a choice, one I thought I would never have to make.

My brother, who looked so helpless in the white frothy waves, but what about my best friend, and the good times we shared!

What was I thinking? I had to save my brother! I prayed and hoped that the water wouldn't knock me out before I got the chance to help him! I jumped in, the shock of the freezing water overwhelmed me but I knew I had to carry on. I grabbed Oliver and managed to pull him onto a nearby cliff.

Then it happened. In the time I had grabbed Oliver, Alice had also managed to climb on to the cliff, and at first I was relieved. But as we were reaching for safety I caught a glimpse of the menace in her eyes, such hatred. Surely she could understand why I chose my brother over her?

Suddenly I felt a hard pounding in my leg and with the pain I lost my grip! I was falling down, down, down into the icy sea.

I swam harder then I had ever swum before, but there was a storm brewing and I stood no chance against the current. Every second I spent in the water I became weaker and weaker, until I had no more strength left. The only thing I remember was Alice's horrible smile as she led screaming Oliver away.

Then I woke up here, wherever here is. As I look around all I can see is a small white room. And as of yet I haven't been able to leave. All I do is sit and wait; I don't even know what I am waiting for! And I could be waiting forever!

Eleanor Dale
Torquay Girls Grammar

EIGHT

In a world where so many lives are being torn apart by divorce and heartache, comes a story of a father and a daughter, and an unspoken promise that was kept.

My father was not a sentimental man. I don't remember him ever 'oo-ing' or 'aah-ing' over something I made as a child. Don't get me wrong; I knew that he loved me in other ways, but getting all mushy-eyed was not his thing.

I learned that he showed his love in other ways. There was one particular time in my life when this became real to me …

I always believed that my parents had a good marriage, but just before I turned eleven, my belief was sorely tested. My father, who used to share in the chores around the house, gradually started becoming despondent. From the time he came home from his job at the pencil factory to the time he went to bed, he hardly spoke a word to my mom or me and my two siblings. The strain on my mom and dad's relationship was very evident. However, I was not prepared for the day that

Mom sat me and my siblings down and told us that Dad had decided to leave. All that I could think of was that I was going to become a product of a divorced family. It was something I never thought was possible. I kept telling myself that it wasn't going to happen, and I went totally numb when I knew my dad was really leaving.

The night before he left, I stayed up in my room for a long time. I prayed and I cried and I wrote a long letter to my dad. I told him how much I loved him and how much I would miss him. I told him that I was praying for him and wanted him to know that, no matter what, I loved him. I wrote that I would always and forever be his daughter and his best friend. As I folded my letter, I stuck in a picture of me with a saying I had heard, 'Anyone can be a father, but it takes a special someone to be a daddy.'

Early the next morning, as my dad left the house, I sneaked out to the car and slipped my letter into one of his bags.

Two weeks went by with hardly a word from my father. Then, one afternoon, I came home from school to find my mom sitting at the dining room table, waiting to talk to me. I could see in her eyes that she had been crying. She told me that Dad had been there and that they had talked for a long time. They decided that there were things that both of them could and would change, and that their marriage was worth saving. Mom then turned her focus to my eyes.

'Isabella, Dad told me that you wrote him a letter. Can I ask what you wrote to him?'

I found it hard to share with my mom what I had written from my heart to my dad. I mumbled a few words and shrugged.

Mom said, 'Well, Dad said that when he read your letter, it made him cry. It meant a lot to him and I have hardly ever seen your dad cry. After he read your letter he called to see if he could come over to talk. Whatever you said really made a difference to your dad.'

A few days later my dad was back, this time to stay. We never talked about the letter, I guess I always figured it was something that was a secret between us.

My parents went on to be married a total of thirty-six years before my dad's early death at the age of fifty-three cut short their lives together. In the last sixteen years of their marriage, all those who knew my mom and dad witnessed one of the truly 'great' marriages. Their love grew stronger every year, and my heart swelled with pride as I saw them grow closer together.

When Mom and Dad received the news from the doctor that Dad's heart was deteriorating rapidly, they took it hand in hand, side by side, all the way.

After Dad's death, we had the most unpleasant task of going through his things. I have never liked this task and opted to run errands so I did not have to be there while most of the things were divided and boxed up. When I got back from my errand, my brother said, 'Izzy, Mom said to give this to you. She said you would know what it meant.'

As I looked down into his outstretched hand, it was then that I knew the impact of my letter that day so long ago. In my brother's hand was my picture that I had given my dad that day. My unsentimental dad, who never let his emotions get the better of him, my dad, who never outwardly showed his love for me, had kept the one thing that meant so much to him and me. I sat down and the tears began to flow, tears that I thought had dried up from the grief of his death, but that had now found new life as I realised what I had meant to him. Mom told me that Dad kept both the picture and the letter his whole life.

I have a box in my home that I call the 'Dad box'. In it are so many things that remind me of him. I pull that picture out every once in a while and remember. I remember a promise that was made many years ago between a young man and his bride on their wedding day, and I remember the unspoken promise that was made between a father and his daughter …

Mia Catton
St Catherine's School, Twickenham

NINE

I should be happy; today's the day I become a teenager. I should be celebrating with Sam, but it's been over a month since anyone's seen him. We were inseparable, but now his parents look at me with sorrow in their eyes. It must be torture not knowing where their son is. I feel their pain, but the difference is that I know where he is and what happened. The guilt is a disease eating away at my body and will keep eating away until they know. It's time to break the promise.

On that day, that plays over and over in my head like a stuck record, the three of us we were outside Sam's, sitting on the cracked kerb, afternoon sun beating down. Bickering about what to do as we always did, we decided to go through the woods, anything to get us out of the sun's beaming rays. Then the forest seemed different, so alive, but the thought of it now chills me to the soul.

Emerging from the daunting growth, we saw the derelict house. Robert opened the heavy iron gate that was hanging off its hinges, the ear-piercing screech of the metal scraping across the chipped paving slabs was deafening. We sauntered across the overgrown garden. Sam noticed that there was a cellar hatch in the ground at the side of the house, which was locked. We were both glad, as neither of us would have wanted to go down there. Robert however would be in like a shot. We decided not to mention it to him.

I leant back against the ice-cold wall, when Robert's voice echoed through the shell of the house, 'Hey guys, c'mon. I found a cellar and I've cracked that code.' Laughing at his own joke. 'Who's going first?'

'I'm not going down there,' protested Sam.

'Oh stop being such a wimp!'

'Yeah,' I agreed, 'you're so boring – just go down there.' I don't even know why I was making him go down, I didn't want to either, but I didn't want Robert to think I was boring. He was a couple of years older than us and everyone at school thought he was cool so, if we knew him, others would think the same about us, but it didn't seem to work like that.

Robert lifted up the hatch door and nudged Sam forward. He reluctantly clambered down the rotten steps. Suddenly there was a loud bark. With that, we all ran and kept on running.

Back at the woods again, I stopped to gain my breath. I sat down in the thick mud and leant back against the withered bark of a tree. I could just see the top of the remains of the house. I pressed my hands into the mud beside me and watched as it clumped around my fingers. I lifted my hand and saw that it had left an imprint on the floor. I looked back towards the house and saw there were only two pairs of footprints. I looked up and saw Robert's face grinning down on me. 'Where's Sam?' I asked.

'I don't know.'

'We need to go back and look for him,' I said.

The sun was setting fast behind the house on the horizon. So we started running back towards the house. We opened up the hatch …

There he was. A huge gash across his forehead. The light from the evening sun reflected off the pool of blood that had once flowed thick and scarlet through his veins and was now spilled across the floor, wasted. Everything was deadly quiet, not even the sound of the birds that were flying back to their nest for the night could be heard. I waited for what seemed like a lifetime for Sam to move but he never did. I dropped to the floor with pear-shaped tears rolling down my cheeks from my bloodshot eyes. My whole body was trembling violently from the shock. I stumbled to my feet and ran, ran like I've never run before. I needed to get help. But I never even made it to the iron gate before Robert grabbed my arms.

'What do you think you're doing? We can't tell anyone about this! They will blame us; they would say we killed him,' he yelled at me.

'It was just an accident,' I protested.

'No it wasn't, you forced him down there,' said Robert.

'What? Don't blame me, you told him to go down there!' I argued. But I was beginning to feel less sure of myself.

'We can't tell anyone, please promise me!' pleaded Robert.

'No. No I won't. That is a human being we are talking about, not a scabby old dog. He is my best friend.' The tears were rolling down faster now and I could hear the terror in my voice, my head was pounding from how hard my body was shaking, I couldn't take any more in.

Robert put his arm around me and said in a very quiet and calm voice, too calm for what had just happened.

'His mother will look at you as if you had killed her

precious son.'

And with that thought now racing round my head I opened my mouth for the fateful words to flow out, 'Fine … fine … I promise.'

We shut the hatch door and we walked away; we never came back.

A month passed and the police were still searching and both of us kept our mouths closed. The guilt was unbearable. Watching Sam's mother walk past my house every morning, with her eyes blotchy and sorrowful, probably going over it in her head every waking moment whether her son was dead, alive, or if he had just run away. The uncertainty must be eating her up inside, because I know the truth and it is tearing me apart. I wish I was the one in the cellar, so that way I wouldn't have to feel this unbearable pain.

Now I think it is time; it has been too long. I can't keep this any more; I have to break the promise.

Kian Taylor
The Holy Trinity C of E Secondary School
Crawley

TEN

Becky Summers hated custard, spiders and slugs, but the thing she hated the most was piano practise. Becky detested practising the piano so much, she often said she would rather be locked in a cell with spiders and forced to bathe in custard for eternity, than play the piano on a regular basis. Unfortunately Becky's parents had other ideas on the piano front; they really wanted Becky to pass her upcoming piano exam with flying colours and they rightly thought the only way to achieve this was through diligent, daily rehearsal.

Becky had previously taken four other piano grades and was currently preparing for her grade five exam which was going to take place in three weeks. She had done well in her earlier exams so everyone thought her mark for grade five would be even better than any of the others. Becky did not work well with this sort of pressure, or any sort of pressure in fact, and if anyone, usually her parents, tried to make her practise, she would try her best to avoid any ounce of help given, especially from her mum (who was a professional pianist) and would retort dramatically if she did not agree with the suggested attempt at improving. One of her many piano avoiding tricks was to tense her fingers and pretend she had robot hands; which hindered rather than helped her playing. Another was to make her homework spread out as long as possible in the evenings, leaving the bare minimum time to practise before being carted off to bed (another daily event she would cause a fiasco about, but that's another story).

Mr and Mrs Summers really wanted to help Becky achieve her full potential at the piano and would argue that it would be a great skill to have in later life, and would have intense discussions late at night when they thought Becky was asleep, though little did they know that she was eavesdropping on every word instead of dreaming sweetly about burning all the pianos in existence in one colossal bonfire.

One particular Saturday morning, Becky had been roused early to practise and had consequently bent two spoons and cracked a breakfast bowl when she was told what she would be spending her day doing. Becky had planned to spend the day completing the final levels of *'Jungle Rocks Earthquake Races'*, a new game that she had been fixed to for every spare, non-piano, second due to its highly realistic, pixelated characters and the beautiful bejewelled controller that she had spent her birthday money on. Becky's parents had planned to make Becky practise at frequent intervals during the day with breaks of half an hour in between each session.

During the scheduled session one of practise, Becky argued and fought with her mother and had her iPod confiscated. During session two, she ripped her manuscript and spat on the keys, causing her new headphones, laptop and chocolate stash to be placed in the dangerous depths of her parents' padlocked confiscation cupboard. Sessions three, four and five didn't go any better, losing Becky her pocket money for two weeks, which was then extended to a month, then extended to six weeks due to Becky hiding dirty socks in the piano, convincing her mum that the practise pedal was stuck. But halfway through Mrs Summers' phone call to the piano tuner, Mr Summers discovered the stash of socks due to the unpleasant stench, reeking from the piano.

By the sixth session, poor Mr Summers had had enough and after a lengthy shouting match with Becky, he made her promise that she would try her hardest and not cause any more piano-related calamities (the insurance company was threatening to take more money if anything else happened to the ancient instrument) and in exchange, Mr and Mrs Summers would promise to reward her if she passed the exam. Becky instantly thought of the latest Play Station Four game *'Jungle Rocks Avalanche Races'* (the sequel to *'Jungle Rocks Earthquake Races'*) and she reluctantly agreed.

Her parents' promise of a reward spurred Becky on and for a few weeks Becky practised industriously every evening, meticulously every morning and she even did the majority of her homework at lunchtime in the library, under the silent reign of the formidable librarian, Madame Bookus.

Becky's parents were thoroughly shocked by their daughter's sudden change of attitude and basked in the beautiful, mistake-free music that emanated from the piano room during Becky's practise. They really should have realised that it was too good to last.

A week before the exam, Becky woke up with a stinking attitude and when practise time came around, she was every parent's idea of torture. She screamed, she shouted, she stamped on her father's foot and changed the colour of her innocent mother's hair dye (Mrs Summers didn't realise the dye was a vile shade of green until she washed it out and it became permanent). Mr Summers, after a large rant at Becky, made her promise to never behave like that again, confiscated *'Jungle Rocks Earthquake Races'* and ran out to the shops to buy the correct hair dye for his wife.

All the time up until the exam Becky was a little angel (she really didn't want to ruin her chances of getting *'Jungle Rocks Avalanche Races'*) and she performed her little heart out in the exam. When the final results came in, it was revealed that Becky had earned a Distinction (the highest mark)!

When the fuss about Becky's mark died down she read the remark sheet and found her favourite comment from the examiner saying: 'This student shows real promise.'

Georgina Gadian
Streatham and Clapham High School

ELEVEN

Flo was just an ordinary girl. She went to school, had friends, and did most things that a eight year old girl would normally do. Flo lived with her father, stepmother, and her older stepsister called Clare who was eighteen. Flo never really spoke to Clare as she was either hidden away in her boring room, or out with her friends. Flo never really understood why Clare wouldn't want to play with her, but would want to play with lots of selfish teenagers.

Most of Flo's time was spent in the shed. Flo's father never understood why she would want to spend her time in such an empty place, but he hadn't stepped inside for over six months, and a lot had happened in the shed since then. Flo had completely revamped the shed on the inside. She had borrowed her father's paint, as her father was a builder, and used it to paint the inside. Her stepmother even installed wooden shelves for her belongings. The shed was with no doubt Flo's favourite place. She had all her toys in there in neat rows along the delicate wooden shelves; she had a bright yellow beanbag on her butterfly rug, which covered the floor. She even had an old television, which was carefully propped up on the wall. The shed was any eight-year-old girl's dream.

Even though she liked to think she loved everything equally and fairly, Flo disliked many things. These were things like broccoli, spiders, heights, and a few other things that didn't really matter, but Flo hated one particular thing, and she didn't just hate it she dreaded it. This was her room. She would use every opportunity she had to avoid her room. Her room to her was like a prison she would never escape. Flo would sometimes sneak in her room in the middle of the day to get her belongings to take to the shed, but apart from that she never went in, except for one time of the day. Bedtime.

Flo's bedroom was the only room in the house that wasn't redecorated when they moved in nine months ago. Her father said it was because it didn't need redecorating and she should stop fussing. No matter how hard she tried, she could not like the room. It had dark floral print wallpaper, with a small window very close to the pale blue ceiling. It had a damp smell and creaky wooden floorboards. It wasn't just that Flo didn't like it, Flo was scared of it. It had a small wooden bed right in the middle or the room, her bed. Her bed was elevated about thirty centimetres off the ground and you could see nothing underneath. Her room also had a dark wardrobe and a large, old, wooden dolls' house, which Flo hadn't touched once, and didn't intend to. It seemed to tower over the room in a sinister fashion, but really it was just a toy.

However, every night Flo would have to quickly run across the floorboards in her pyjamas, trying to step on the ones that she thought wouldn't creak and would then quickly hop into bed and make sure her whole body was covered by the duvet. Almost every single night Flo would hear noises, see shapes, and see tiny things in the corner of her eye moving in her room. Flo was petrified. Flo was certain that she wasn't the only thing in her room. Her father would have to come in every night since they moved in and make the same promise. He would say, 'I promise the monsters in your room aren't real, nothing will hurt you or attack you in your sleep and, most of all, remember it is all in your head.' No matter how many times she was told this Flo still hated her bedroom, but that promise still made her feel a lot safer than she was without it.

The more she tried to figure out what the odd figures and shapes were, the more she saw. The more she saw, the closer they would get to her. Every night there would be strange noises in her room like the wind howling, wood creaking and the grandfather clock in the corner ticking, but there was one noise that she could not stand. It came from the dolls' house. It was a sort of muffled sound that sounded to Flo a bit like giggling, every month it seemed to get louder and louder. Flo was so terrified of the dolls' house she would never go near enough to find out what it was.

After a while of Flo complaining about the room, her father had had enough and gave her a long and stern lecture about how she needed to grow up. Then Flo got extremely lucky. Clare said she could have her room whilst she was at university. Flo couldn't believe her luck. She would finally get her own proper room and wouldn't have to be scared of it. Clare went away for four years and over this period Flo's fear for her old room started to go away. All of her belongings that were in the shed were now in her room and Flo couldn't have been happier.

When Clare came back from university, she planned on staying at home for one more year whilst she was finding a job. Flo agreed to move back into her old room. Flo was no longer scared or petrified of her room. It was just a normal place in the house to her now. Flo didn't even need her father to promise her that she would be okay overnight. As it was summer, Flo wasn't afraid to sleep without the covers on. Flo shut her eyes and went to sleep.

The next morning, Flo's father woke up, and brought Flo breakfast in bed. To his surprise, when he stepped in Flo's room, Flo was gone. So was the dolls' house.

Isla Patterson
St Catherine's School, Twickenham

TWELVE

Tears were brewing in my eyes as a dark metallic green truck pulled up in our drive, there were men chatting and joking in the back. A tall bald man slowly walked up to our front door, by this time tears were streaming down my face. The officer was heavily built and as he brought his hand up to knock on the door, I saw tattoos on his arms and some creeping up his neck. His firm knock echoed around the room and we all knew that it was time. We hugged for so long that the officer had to pull us apart. Dad looked at me, his warm, shaky hands wrapped around my head. He said solemnly, 'I'll be back, I promise.' I ran up the stairs, to the nearest window and pressed my face against the cold glass. He had gone and all I had left of him was his footprints left in the gravel.

Mother became really depressed and often I had to look after her; days got longer and seemed to drag on. I had no one to look forward to playing football with and no one to cheer me up in the evenings. It was not the same.

After a long month, I started to get used to it, I forgot about Dad and just pretended he was still here, this was until we got the letter. It came in a pale pink, faded envelope, and it had a real seal. I had just come back from school and was checking on Mother. Mother opened it, hands shaking, her tears dripping onto the ink, making it run. The letter read:

Dear Mrs Jamieson,

May I be permitted to express my own and the squadron's sincere sympathy with you in the sad news concerning your husband. The aircraft of which he was the flight engineer took off to attack Trossy St. Maximin Constructional Works, near Paris on the 24th April 1945, and nothing further has been heard.

You may be aware that in quite a large percentage of cases aircrew reported missing are eventually reported prisoners of war, and I hope that this may give you some comfort in your anxiety. Once again please accept the deep sympathy ...

I could not read any more, I wanted to smash something or break something. My hand reached out for the door and before I knew what I was doing I was heading towards the shed. I flung open the door and retrieved an old rusty bicycle. Mother was chasing after me, I felt bad but I could not take her pain and sadness any longer.

There were no lights on the road, it was like I was riding into blackness, I pedalled all through the night, I did not care where I was going, but I was going to find him.

A sudden crackling awoke me, I opened my eyes to a fire and an old-looking gentleman. He extended his wrinkled hand and in it was a cup of hot milk. I was wrapped in a patchy blanket and was lying on a brown-coloured sofa; it looked like I had been consumed by its cushions. I did not know where I was. Hurriedly, I asked as calmly as possible who he was. He replied and kindly told me that he was on his night shift, at the railway depot when he spotted me, asleep in the waiting room with a bicycle. He told me his name was Harry and before he could say anything else, my eyes felt heavy again and closed giving up to the warmth.

The next morning Harry asked me where I lived, I told him where. I did not want to go back as I needed to find my dad. I told him I was at the station hoping to catch a train to France when he found me. I explained everything. Harry told me that he would walk me home, my mother would be worried.

Rays of light beamed down on us, it was a balmy May morning. People were cheerful, everyone seemed so happy. Or maybe I was just sad. Harry explained to me that my dad is doing a great thing; he is serving our wonderful nation. He is an honourable man, he told me, I should be proud and live up to what my dad has done for our country. This was true, and it made me feel less miserable. As we approached the village I was glad to see familiar surroundings, but something seemed odd. People hugged and kissed, ran around singing, the static sound of tuning a wireless was played out of many houses. The sounds were a blur so I kept walking.

After ten minutes of walking we arrived at my house. 'Here it is.'

I thanked Harry politely for all he had done for me. He shook my hand and told me to be positive and hopeful. I dropped my bicycle and knocked on the door. To my amazement my mother opened it fully dressed in her Sunday best. Before I could react she hugged me tight and told me never to do that again. I could make out tears on her face; Mother let go, she was like her old self.

'So, have you heard?'

I replied, 'No, about what?'

'The war is over!' she cried. 'The Germans surrendered, we are safe.' Momentarily, it seemed she had forgotten about Dad. She looked me in the eye and told me to be strong.

I went up to my room, looked out of the window, up at the sky. Dad promised he would be back, maybe he will, I imagined him, walking up the gravel; he'll be back, I know it.

Louis Partridge
Dulwich Prep London

THIRTEEN

Open up! Open up!
They screamed through the whole of our ghetto. They charged inside the house where my mother and my father, and sister and brother, and what else was left of my family were. They grabbed us so hard my arm was nearly dislocated. They said we were going to a better place. Anywhere was better than our ghetto, where dead bodies littered everywhere and the stench was horrendous. We had no radio to listen to. We barely had any food. Anywhere would be better than our ghetto.

About thirty of us were squashed into the back of a van. It was dirty and covered in blood and mud, much like the films I had sneaked into the cinema to watch, years ago. We sat on our suitcases so we didn't get covered in mud. We came to a halt at the train station. Fifty of us were pushed into a carriage. There was no air to breathe. It was stifling, but I couldn't move to even take my coat off. The train wasn't like the ones that we went on when we went on holiday; they had comfortable chairs, but we had none at all. The journey took about an hour and thirty minutes but that's not a fact. There were no clocks.

The train stopped and my hand could not grip any tighter on my mother; the only person who could get it off was the soldier. We were separated, men and women. The babies were snatched from their mothers. Our suitcases were taken off us. Our watches were taken off us. Our clothes were taken off us. They were substituted with itchy pyjamas that stunk of horse manure. I did the wrong thing, breathing through my nose. I was starting to think that our ghetto was actually better, which I would never have imagined before.

Our huts were covered in mud and there were five of us lying in a single bed. One was a boy called Amir, and although he got more miserable as the days went on, we sort of clicked. He was almost a brother. In the spare time we had, we would always talk to each other. We didn't talk while we worked though as we would have been whipped by the soldiers. It looked like it hurt – the same man kept getting it done. I always cringed because he looked like he was going through excruciating pain. I always did what I was told by the soldiers as I didn't want to get whipped.

There were the toilets which I didn't go to; it was only a cement slab with holes in. It smelt like a pig sty and made me vomit in my mouth. I wished I could see my mother because she could always make a silent moment break into sudden laughter. I loved it back at home where my mother used to make the best *challah*. I just needed food. I could see myself getting thinner by the day, my ribs were becoming more prominent. I could not go another day without food, and while I risked death stealing it, I'd die anyway without it.

The hut where we got the food from was always unguarded at the same time every day when the soldiers had their break. It would be the perfect time to go get some food, but I couldn't let anyone see me break the rules or else I would be in a lot of trouble with the soldiers. So this was the hardest choice of my life. If I went, I wouldn't be in pain any more and I wouldn't be so skinny. But I could end my life and never see another day. What was I going to do? What would the choice be? Choices, choices …

This was the day when my plan was going to turn into a reality. My talks with Amir could wait. I needed the food. I had made the biggest choice of my life. I should just go for it and feel the guilt later. The bell had rung when it was time for the break for the soldiers; this was my chance. I had to be as quiet as a mouse and make myself invisible. The hut seemed further away than usual. I tiptoed my way towards it, towards the bread and apples and the water fountain outside. It felt, it tasted, like heaven. The bread filled a hole in my stomach, the apple was so juicy. All I needed was a drink of water from the fountain outside to wash it all down.

I tiptoed backwards to make sure nothing was coming from the other doors. But as I turned around, there were polished shoes, starched pants, pressed shirt, a blazer and a very shiny hat crested with a sign with four legs. The gun seemed to be stuck against his thigh. I knew I was in big trouble. He dragged me by the neck, took me to his office. My heart was pumping like it never had before. He said that I had breached the rules and I would certainly be punished. But I hadn't expected what happened next.

They guided me to a wooden platform with a tall rectangular frame around it. They lifted me onto the platform. I thought I could see a trapdoor beneath me. They put a tight rope around my neck, and a bag over my head.

The door dropped.

My organs stopped.
My pulse disappeared.
I hope this torture will never be done on any person again.

Ryan Krzyzaniak
St Edmund Arrowsmith
Ashton-in-Makerfield

FOURTEEN

A small girl huddled in the corner of the dark, dusty room crying into a small dirty rag which she started wrapping around her hand. She had been alone in the dust-infested room for a day without a bit to eat or a phone call from any one. She looked into the empty darkness of the room … wait, it was not empty, the letter was still there on the kitchen table – blood red writing and all. She shook her head as if to shake the image out of her mind. She paused and looked to each side of her. Nervously she tried her phone again, she pressed it urgently to her ear. She heard a dull beeping coming from the other side. Suddenly the beeping sound stopped.

'Pick up, Mum, please,' whispered Sarah.

A voice came back on. 'Sorry, Danielle is not available at the moment. Please leave a message after the tone.' A dull beep filled the breathless air around her and she heard the sound of footsteps down the passage.

Sarah knew she had not much time left. She pushed her phone to her mouth and in an urgent whisper said: 'I know I will probably be dead by the time you get this, but this morning a man shoved me into his car and drove off and I now have no idea where I am and I am all alone in a dark dirty room, but please help me and get this message in time.'

The footsteps were getting louder. They reached the door and a muffled grunt of effort filled the air whilst the lock turned in the door – if you could call the big metal monstrosity a door that is. It looked as if you could contain the most dangerous wild animal behind it; or perhaps a criminal, a killer. Nails and long metal spikes stuck out at every angle. She had not planned or tried an escape and nor was she going to, not with that door in the way.

The door swung open and as if in unison a loose floorboard flipped up and Sarah's phone was shoved roughly in.

The sound of a light switch was heard throughout the room and all the doom and gloom of the room was illuminated in a small dusty glow whilst a skeletal white face loomed in the shadows.

His face just millimetres from Sarah's ear, he cackled, 'Are we missing Mummy? Are we scared? Would you like something to eat or maybe something to drink?'

One thousand questions raced through her mind as Sarah stammered, 'What d-d-do you want with me-e? What a-are you going to-o do with me?'

A piercing screech of a voice filled Sarah's ears. 'You want to know, do you really want to know what I want to do with you? Well, I will tell you this. There is no way into here and neither is there any way out.'

The strange man seemed to slither to the door but at the door he stopped and said, 'I feel your Mummy may be drawing her final breath too.'

And with that he vanished, but his words didn't. They rang in Sarah's ears as clear as a bell and in vain she shouted after him, 'What have you done to her, have you done it yet, please tell me, and tell her I am sorry and that I never meant what I wrote in that letter.' There was no answer but a cackle in return.

Sarah looked at her watch. It was 12 o'clock at night. She found the softest and safest bit of floor she could, and curled up in a small ball of coldness and shut her eyes, anxious to go to sleep, to escape from the world of cruelty and horror, and most of all THE MESSAGE – she had left on the kitchen table the day before in the morning. It said: 'I am never talking to you again after what you said to me last night, so I thought it would be best if I went away, far away.'

Sarah was asleep at last, having a dream. Her mum was at the door trying to get her. Sarah rushed forward, trying to reach her. Slowly the dream started to turn into a nightmare. Her mum drew her hand away and started laughing, or to be more accurate, she was cackling, cackling like a witch – pointing, staring then crying, holding out the message. She dropped it then left her there, her footsteps fading into the darkness. Sarah was screaming: 'NO! Don't leave! Mum, come back!'

Sarah awoke suddenly with a jolt. She sat up immediately, looking at the door. No one was there but she could hear someone coming … He was back. 'Hello there dearie,' he shrieked, did you sleep well? Answer me!'

Sarah sat there in stunned silence. How did that happen? She was hanging from the ceiling by her hair, how could she not have noticed? She blinked again, she was on the floor and she blinked again. 'What is happening to me?' she said to herself.

The man said: 'I am an illusionist. Have you ever heard the term?'

Sarah gasped and stuttered, 'But how do I know what is real and what isn't, or if any of this is real at all.'

The man came closer and whispered, just so she could hear. 'The answer is simple, you don't.'

Isabelle Owen
St. Catherine's School, Twickenham

FIFTEEN

It simply said, 'GET ME OUT OF HERE, I AM GOING CRAZY!'

He had hundreds of the same message, scribbled on some faded notepaper with 'Prince's Hospital' stamped on it. It might just be a prank, after all, the Prince's Hospital was a place full of loonies. But, how did the notes get here?

This thought had made him slightly more on edge as he went to his next assignment. It was late, but he was just meant to check the ward, and spend the night there, as there were some suspicions that the warden was giving patients something to make them more 'compliant'.

The man had done this kind of visit so many times now, and wished, instead of becoming an expert in studying 'the mind', the false promise of an interesting life, that he had chosen a different path. A surgeon maybe; at least a surgeon would occasionally save some lives.

He rapped on the door. A middle-aged, but weary-looking man opened. He led him into a vast room, with only a plain carpet and a big cold fireplace. There was a sign, which was covered in cobwebs and was in danger of falling off, which said, 'WELCOME TO PRINCE'S HOSPITAL.'

The warden, Jones, seemed to share about the same affection for the place as the sign. 'Welcome to Prince's Hospital,' he muttered, like a squirrel which had lost its nut. He waved his hand in the direction of a chair. The chair was wooden and it slouched as the legs on the right were bent, and so the psychiatrist had to really lean to one side to avoid being knocked off the chair. The warden walked into the room marked 'STAFF ONLY' and came out again and passed the psychiatrist some tea in a dusty mug. It tasted foul, and bitter.

'So, how can I help?' the warden asked uninterestedly. His breath was stinking of a smell not unfamiliar to the psychiatrist. The psychiatrist's last office had smelled permanently of this as the office next to him had belonged to a coroner.

'Yes, I have been informed by my superiors of one particular patient who, apparently, might have been given a 'special' treatment as he was sometimes … uncontrollable.'

The warden seemed to think about this for too long, and then he replied, 'I know nothing of this, would you care to give me the name of this patient please?'

The psychiatrist looked in his notes. 'Um, his name is Alex McDonald.'

'Oh, Alex,' he said, as if it was a private joke. 'Okay, this way please.'

He led the way, and stopped outside room 109. He opened the door, but no-one was there. There was everything that you would expect, a basin, a bed, and a barred window. But there was one thing missing – the patient himself.

The warden however seemed to think that this was not the case.

'Hello Alex,' he said.

There was an imaginary response and then the warden nodded and said, 'Okay, I'll leave you to it then.'

He closed the door, and then said to the psychiatrist, 'Better not to disturb him now.'

The psychiatrist was stunned, the message now suddenly loomed large in his head.

The old ward was much darker now, and looked even more sinister, as if it had its own secrets to hide. Without another word, the warden showed him his room for the night. It was better equipped than room 109, but it was still very simple and dirty.

Somewhere there was a rhythmical thumping, or was it from his head? It was already dark and he felt, for once, afraid of this place. He glanced out of the window; he could swear he saw someone on the cliff opposite the ward, doing a crucifixion action, and then all too quickly he just jumped off. The psychiatrist tried to shout, but everything just went black.

Next thing he knew, he was lying on the floor. Clutched in his hand was a crumpled piece of paper. Another message, or was it the old one? Absent-mindedly, he put it in his coat pocket. Thoughts rummaged through his head, about the events last night, and the patient incident. Was everyone here crazy, even the warden, talking to imaginary people? And who was the man on the cliff? Was he the missing Alex?

He raced through the wards looking for the warden, and suddenly realised that he couldn't really see anyone else. There were no nurses, no other patients, only the warden. He nearly bumped into him going round one of the ward's many corridors.

'How was your night then?' the warden asked.

'Fine, and yours?' he said automatically, trying to

calm his own nerves.

'Very good actually,' the warden replied. 'So, you want to talk to Alex now?'

The dull thumping had grown consistently stronger and it was getting harder to focus on the warden's words.

'Yes, I would, thank you.'

He led the psychiatrist through the maze of the ward. They stopped outside room 109 again.

'Hello Alex, someone here wants to speak with you.'

The psychiatrist went in, but it was still empty! What was wrong with this warden? He was obviously playing a game with him, but what, and why?

'Warden, a moment please,' he said.

The warden came over. 'Yes, what is it?'

'What is going on?' he asked. He could no longer contain his rising panic.

The warden replied, 'What do you mean?'

'Where is Alex? I can't see anyone in here and yet you talk to him as if he is. And where is everybody? This place is deserted! I can only see you in the whole of this ward. No nurses, no assistants, no other patients, nothing!'

The warden sighed, and shook his head as if really disappointed in what he had said. He then muttered, 'It didn't work. I thought I had it.'

The psychiatrist was mystified. 'What do you mean, it didn't work. What didn't work?'

The warden sighed, and said, 'You, Alex.'

John James Daley
Dulwich Prep London

SIXTEEN

It was a promise.

My gran died a couple of years ago. I was inconsolable. I loved her so much because she was my very best friend. One of the things I adored about her was that she was a connoisseur on calling people by the completely wrong name, like she would call me Bobby or Jenny. Another thing she would do was keep a secret stash of Snickers at the bottom of her wardrobe and make me go out and by her another three packets of them, so she had a wardrobe full of them. She loved chocolate, even more than she LOVED syrup and porridge in the morning, and she loved syrup! The funniest thing that happened was at her last birthday (96th birthday). My dad poured her a lovely cup of non-spilling tea, which then she kept spilling all over her blue and black sequinned from head to toe skirt. So then one of the ladies from the care home came to join us for Gran's birthday. She quite liked my brother as she would constantly be following him around trying to play with his curly blond and beautiful hair; bearing in mind he was six, you can't just expect a six-year-old to go with the flow and not try to escape from an old freaky lady trying to touch his curly blond and beautiful hair!

A few months later she died. She died of old age. I ran to her room in the care home, 28, first corridor, bottom floor; as you can probably tell, I can still and always will remember that number. Her bed had been stripped and the sheets taken away, her belongings were being packed and stored.

A letter. There on her baby-blue background, flower-printed bedside table, a letter. I tentatively grabbed the letter and shoved it in my pocket. It was addressed to me, promise. I was still so melancholy that I couldn't even bear to think about my best friend dying, never mind the letter! It took me exactly 1 month, 2 weeks, 4 days, 7 hours and 52 seconds to eventually open the letter. I was petrified. I didn't want to think of her death, I wanted to be able to share the Snickers with her and also the box of Celebrations, which I obviously didn't tell you about because I swore not to say anything.

I could hear the stickiness of the lip of the envelope as I carefully peeled it off with cautiousness. What would it say? When had she written it? Did she know she was going to die? Where is she? I miss her. I could feel the sour, salty tears running like a torrent of sadness down my face. Droplets of bravery, determination, courageousness fell like an autumn leaf onto the envelope. My heart was racing as fast as Lewis Hamilton speeding round the track!

My imagination was running wild. Maybe it could be that she wants me to take up reading as more of a hobby, then again she did love reading! Or maybe it was that she wants me to stop eating Snickers so that she wouldn't miss out on the chocolate. Oooh ooh, it could be that she wants me to travel the world and swim with dolphins as she never got the opportunity to do so. Oh, I really wish she was here to do it with me. Why did she have to live in the olden times uurrgghh! Back to the letter. I had to coax myself to pull out the letter. I could feel the lump in my throat growing bigger and bigger as I slowly pulled it out. I was holding it hard in my hand. It was cartridge paper, just how I remember, as she always used that paper. As soon as I read the first line I felt a shiver rush down my spine. It was ten lines of different promises, and it looked like this:

Promise me you will always buy 3 packets of Snickers a week and eat mine for me (so I was wrong about the not eating Snickers and her missing out on them).

Promise me you will read all of my books and enjoy them.

Promise me you travel the world.

Promise me you will swim with dolphins (I was right about that).

Promise me you will always be a good sister.

Promise me to follow your heart not always your head.

Promise to come and talk to me most often.

Promise me you will visit the theatre as much as you can.

Promise me to always follow your dreams and never give up.

And most of all promise me to never stop smiling.

As soon as I set my eyes on these promises I knew I just had to keep them! Every week I bought 3 packets of Snickers, I read many of her books, *Pride and Prejudice*, *Oliver Twist*, and a range of classics. I hope and think I have been a good sister, but I have not managed to travel the world or swim with dolphins, yet. And I will never, ever stop smiling!

I really hate being told what to do, but these promises

weren't something that did that. They were special and they are something that I want to do for my best friend. I love visiting my gran even though she may not physically be there. I loved her so much and always will. Gran, I just want to say, 'You are the best gran, the best chocoholic and most importantly … the best, best friend anyone could ever have. Love you, Gran.'

Maddison Pick
Gateways School, Leeds

SEVENTEEN

I ran. I forced my feet to pound one in front of the other. I fixed my eyes on the trees ahead of us. Focusing on my breathing, I breathed in a sharp painful breath. Faster. I kept on running, never stopping. The rain clawed at my already sweat-drenched clothing. I pushed away the thoughts of jealousy, hatred and death that clouded my vision, and focused on what lay ahead of us. Don't look back. I couldn't look back. My heart was pounding against my empty chest, my lungs felt like they were going to burst but I still ran on. Faster. I could hear Tate's low breathing and heavy footsteps beside me. He gave me a flash of his white crooked teeth that tugged into a grim smirk. I smiled back at him almost in slow motion, and then I snapped my head back forward and ran.

There were no words between us, we didn't need to say anything, and we both knew where we were going. Up the hill, turn a right, then a left, enter the woods and then follow the line of oak trees, we were there. We stopped suddenly, clasping our knees, whilst shudders were rolling off our spines, taking in ragged shallow breaths, in, out, in, out. We looked up at each other both recognizing the understanding in our matching cold grey eyes. We didn't look the same, but we had the same eyes, they were the colour of the sea before a storm, the colour of the moon just before dusk. We had that deep silent understanding between two brothers, Blood Brothers.

My eyes followed Tate's movements as he slowly bent down, burying his grime-covered hand into his mud-splattered sock retrieving a penknife. He flipped it open with a fluent flick of his wrist letting the delicate moonlight glisten in the harsh blade. He silently beckoned me forward and I did so obediently. He cautiously placed the penknife in my hand. I slowly closed my palm bringing my hand into a tight fist. It was as if I was watching what we were doing from outside of my own body.

A sharp pang of pain brought me back to my senses, the pain was caused by a shallow cut that appeared on my palm. A metallic smell filled my nostril as beads of blood snaked down my wrist in a slow steady trickle. I delicately gave the penknife back to Tate as he repeated the action. We then lifted out hands up almost simultaneously, inches apart but not yet touching.

'We will forget what happened tonight. We will never speak of this to another soul,' Tate stressed.

'We will try to forget, but we will never forgive them and never doubt that what we did was the right thing to do,' I grunted.

'They deserved it,' said Tate with a tired smile in his voice.

'I promise,' we both said with a smirk and a sinister wink. We grabbed each other's hands and squeezed tightly never looking away from each other's eyes. Letting our blood fuse together to make a blood promise.

I remember that day as if it were yesterday. The day I will never be able to take back, the day that replays in my mind every time I close my eyes, the day I will never forget, the day where it all went wrong.

I have been locked up for 725 days, 6 hours and 14 seconds now. I have nothing but the angry voices in my head, stone walls, the sounds of sadness and nothing to keep me company. I hate those voices, but part of me agrees with them.

All I have is four walls, four walls filled with loneliness and sadness. This place, this prison, this living personal hell has become my life, everything I know, my every second. Almost two years. I am surprised I lasted this long.

I haven't spoken for 725 days. I have been screaming inside of my head since I arrived here but no one ever hears me. I remember the first day I walked into this prison, I finally felt the guilt that had been buried inside me for so many years, the grief over Tate's death, the magnitude of our weak and naïve decisions and promises, our poor judgement, just everything. There are no words to describe the sadness and hurt that I still feel. And that is the reason why I silently cry myself to sleep every single night.

This prison has drained me, emotionally and physically, but there is one thing that has helped me get through this, helped me to survive. It's a technique that I have learnt from staying here. A scheme, a bluff, a deception, a trick. First of all you need to avoid showing emotions associated with weakness, including sadness and fear. I learnt that the nights are the worst, that's when the sadness seeps through the protective emotional wall that you have built around you. I also learnt that this is just one big game, and only the tough survive, and that in every game there is always a trick, a cheat.

The cheat is to not care, to not care about the pain and what your actions have caused, the cheat is to not care about anything. The trick of not caring is important; it's the only way to survive in a place like this. Knowing this has helped keep me from losing my mind altogether, but some days, most days, every day, I wonder why I insist on keeping myself alive.

All of this, this prison, this sadness and this grief were all caused by one action, and one single promise we made to cover it. The promise that destroyed my life, destroyed and killed my best friend and destroyed all of my hope. But now I understand that promises are always broken.

Caitlin Piper
St Catherine's School, Twickenham

EIGHTEEN

A dismal, prison-grey sky lingers over the landscape, obscuring the warm rays of amber light from the ground. Trees stand motionless on the horizon, untouched by the slackened wind; they are almost colourless, the few remaining leaves shivering in the cold, or lying in mounds below. Robins flutter into life, early in the morning, disturbing the thick layers of snow that had formed overnight. However, nature is cut off by a threatening, towering titanium wall, topped with curls of electrified barbed wire. There have been incidents where a lone deer or stag naively attempts to jump this wall, in search of food or water. Their burnt carcasses hang from the wire, or rest on the ground, caked in snow. There are only two ways in or out of the wall: through a ten inch thick gate that can only be opened by key card, or hovercraft.

'Mykael!' My uncle beckons me from the empty window frame, and I have to drag my arms from a woodlouse-eaten windowsill to face him. A rugged man with a chestnut brown beard, partly veiled by a fresh sheet of snow, stands before me. Waterfalls of curled dark hair topple over his head, flicked out of his eyes, their warm hazel somewhat drawing attention from his rough appearance.

My uncle is well known for his rebellious attitude to authority in our region, Sector 9, and the ridiculous laws they enforce so cruelly. The strictest of these include: stealing, hunting without a permit, murder, damaging property that belongs to the government, venturing outside of the wall of our region, or, most illegal of all, disgracing the tyrannical and fanatical dictator of the sectors, Principle Kupe. If any of these laws are broken, the punishments can be as strict as being flogged in the middle of the town square, or ultimately, death by firing squad.

The most odd and badly thought out of these is the hunting without a permit law, as barely anyone can afford a hunting permit and even if you can, the only animals within the wall that aren't domesticated are birds or squirrels. Many people starve to death for this very reason. The rations that the government provide are not enough to support one person, let alone families.

Despite my uncle's tendency for law breaking, he is a caring and loving man, so much so, that when my parents died from a virus, he comforted me, protected me, and treated me as his own. He promised them that he would take care of me if anything ever happened to them, and he has kept that promise ever since.

'Uncle!' I exclaim. I rush into his warm embrace.

'How are you Mykael, are you well? Have you eaten?' He always bombards me with questions about my well-being.

'I'm fine, have you?'

'Yes, I ate at the black market.' I recall my first time at the black market, an illegal market of stalls and cheap necessities, such as food and medicine, and even switchblades, for a hefty price. Weapons are not allowed in the Sector. The Government has always had a fear of rebellion, or uprising.

'Come with me, I need to show you something.'

I slip on my worn denim jacket. It's too ragged and thin to protect me from the bite of the cold, and I've been wearing it since I was ten, but it's all I have. The tall, muscular man hauls a grey bag onto his shoulders. He slams the withered door to our home shut, and the door frame explodes in a cloud of dust and wood shavings. In the markets, further into Sector 9, the shop owners can afford proper houses. Here, in the outskirts, we own claustrophobic wooden structures, built upon muddied stone structures. This is how almost everyone in Sector 9 lives, wallowing in slums.

The street is swarming with people, most under-dressed for the winter cold. Unlike us, they are far too poor to afford even the cheapest, most essential clothing. They normally die by the end of the season. In the distance, I can just distinguish the mountain range that sits upon the edge of the wall. I know what lies upon the cliffs. All of the lower classes, men and women, are required to work at the dam. It is crafted of hard concrete, with many futuristic white pods built nearby. The control rooms. They remain clean and untouched by our grimy hands. Only scientists, officials, or operators are granted access to their prestigious contents. We peasants merely conduct repairs, build generators, or improve the dam. If any person over sixteen does not attend the hydraulics dam every day (except Sunday), he would be hunted down by sentries and receive twenty public lashings. I shudder at the thought.

A squad of sentries turn the corner, shoving past a group of huddling innocents. Their glossy black helmets glisten in the light, their faces disguised by blacked out visors. Suits of thin body armour wrap around their figures, military brown and jet black in colouring. Small bags hang from their backs, carrying gear and ammunition. I catch a glimpse of their guns: huge, white weapons with long steel barrels that are coated in red paint. Red, so that blood doesn't stain the barrel. I've seen an execution before, and if I can help it, I never want to be staring down the barrel of their guns when they go off. The bullets travel faster than usual in their guns.

After the sentries have passed, Uncle and I sprint down an alleyway, rushing to get to our destination. There are a pair of cellar doors at the end. His large, masculine hands seize the handles, yellow rust crumbling into his fingers. He heaves them open.

I hear marching, the sentries are coming.

'Mykael, run through the tunnel. I made a promise to your parents, and I'm not about to break it!' He shoves me in and seals the doors. The sentries are here.

Bang!

Danny Matten
The Holy Trinity C of E Secondary School
Crawley

NINETEEN

Edward squeezed the tears back under his eyelids, trying desperately to force a smile onto his face and look cheerful. He was determined they wouldn't see his misery. Stumbling after them down the cliffs he noticed the clouds growing darker and heavier. How utterly ridiculous and Scottish, he thought, to be going picnicking in this dismal weather.

'Come on Ed, keep up. Remember to collect some wood for the fire!' his cousin Dougal yelled into the wind. They were trying to be kind but Edward knew they were fed up of him already. He had heard Aunt Mary explaining to them that his father might lose his leg. Just hearing someone voice his worst fears had been awful. He was so angry about it all. Why had Dad been a hero and gone back to help someone else? It had been nearly end of his tour in Helmand and he should have just stayed safe. Edward hadn't even been allowed to see him in the hospital, because Mum had decided that she should go first and he should go to Scotland. He wanted to try and cheer Dad up, not be sent away to 'have fun' with family he hardly knew. Edward just hated being here.

He trudged after the others. There was a small gaggle of boys already on the beach.

'Hey Ed, come and meet Finn. You'll like him, he's really cool,' shouted Dougal.

This worried Edward, as most 'really cool' people he had met were bullies and thoroughly unpleasant. Finn looked like the kind of boy Dougal would think was cool. He was big and muscular and wearing Converse boots and long shorts as if this was a basketball court rather than a pebble beach.

Finn called out, 'Hey, dude, come down here!' Edward just muttered a shy 'hello' without really looking up.

'Come on everybody, let's start making the food,' called Aunt Mary over-cheerfully.

A few days later Edward was reading his book in the park when he heard the boys again. 'Hey, Ed, is it, you wanna come an' have a fag?' Finn called out.

'No, not really,' Edward stuttered.

'Aw, come on!' said the rest of the gang.

'Come on guys, he doesn't have to if he doesn't want to.' The gang trooped past. They nodded at him as they went past. He told them that he might come when he had finished the chapter, but the book he was reading didn't have chapters. 'They say his dad's a war hero but you'd never know. He seems gutless,' the boy with spiky red hair remarked in an over-loud whisper.

As the summer dragged on, Edward became obsessed with the gang, wanting to join in but never daring to. He plotted their movements and soon his close observation meant that he could predict their movements before they had even decided on them themselves. Today he had gone to the old bothy, one of their favourite smoking places, and was sitting on an old tree stump, reading and watching out of the corner of his eye. They didn't even see him went they went in. A few minutes later, they trooped out of the bothy.

'Hey, Ed, why've you been spying on us?' demanded the one they called Ginge.

'What, no, why would I spy on you? I'm just reading my book,' Edward replied calmly.

'Well I've seen you "just reading your book" quite a lot recently. So I'm asking you to stop following us, okay, and go and read your book somewhere else.' This was a long speech for the gang and Ginge looked really pleased with himself. They strutted off, and Edward slunk down the other way. He wandered around for a bit. But they had used the bothy, why couldn't he? He scrambled back up the slope and soon the bothy was in sight.

They had made a real mess round there, leaving empty bottles lying around everywhere outside their den. Edward had a sudden feeling that something was wrong. Finn hadn't been with the gang. He was always with them. Where could he be? Then he saw smoke seeping out from under the broken old door of the bothy. He pushed the door open and coughed on the thick, heavy smoke.

'Quick, help!' he screamed, 'Fire, fire!' There was nobody around to hear; no one to help him. If Finn was in there, he was going to have to save him alone. He steeled himself, took some deep breaths and charged through to the room at the back of the hut. The hot flames were myriad colours and had already consumed most of the bothy. He couldn't see Finn but was sure he was there. His eyes streaming, he dropped down to the ground and blindly felt his way across the room. He bumped into a body, took hold of it and dragged it over to the doorway. The roof fell in over the room at the back and he knew it would not be long before the rest of it came down too. He had to get Finn out. He shouted at him to wake up but just ended up taking a lungful of smoke and coughing furiously. The heat was so intense now that he just had to get out immediately. With a huge heave, he tugged Finn over the threshold and rolled him down the slope. He collapsed to the ground and saw nothing else.

He wasn't aware of anything much for the next couple of days, but woke up in hospital, with his mum there holding a phone out to him: 'It's Dad for you.'

'Hey, Dad! How are you?'

'Better than I was. How are you, hero?'

'I'm not a hero, Dad. I knew there was someone in there, I didn't have a choice.'

'There's always a choice, son. You just made the right one.'

Tom King
Dulwich Prep London

TWENTY

You fell asleep and the world flashed in front of your eyes; you saw tall waves, rolling hills, sandy deserts. You fell asleep and dreamt of bright colours, flashing lights, the rumble of thunder.

Your eyes snapped open and you took a sharp breath. You were sweating all over and tangled in your thin bedsheets. He promised that you could see it all. That you could watch the tall waves fall over each other and travel over the sandy deserts on camel-back. But then he was diagnosed and you had to promise him that he would make it, that everything was going to be ok. And then you promised each other you would never give up hope.

And then he died. And you died inside.

Mother wouldn't talk to you any more. She just sat in her chair and stared at the picture on the mantelpiece of their wedding day. It was surrounded by precious memories but she only looked at the golden one, when he was young and healthy and her face was full of happiness. You cried frantically and mourned for him but she would never say a word, yet tears frequently

streamed down her face. On his funeral d₂
dress her into a long black dress and trie
up, but you gave up after she started ₁
despite your gentle ways. During the servic
in the front row, tears streaming down ₁
whilst everyone who had known him made a
contribution to the ceremony. You made a speech, a long
one, about your childhood and your favourite memories
with him. You tried to keep going through the whole
thing but every time you looked at Mother, you had to
stop reading to take a calming breath. You were crying
when you read the last line.

You hoped it would get better, but it never did and she
didn't say a word for days after the funeral. After what
seemed like forever, she started to function properly but
she was never herself again. After the funeral, that night
you woke sweating all over and tangled in your thin bedsheets, you had seen his face in your dreams promising
you that one day, you would travel the world together
and see all there was to see. You saw his ill face and
heard your own voice promising it was going to be
alright. But he was dead and there was nothing you
could do about it.

The day after the nightmare you visited your favourite
place in the world. You had discovered it together and
had sat there for hours, watching the sunset. You lived
on the coast of Cornwall but you never knew you were
this close to water. The cliff was on the edge of the
evergreen woodland and your village was on the other
side of it. You knew all the moods of the place;
throughout the year it seemed as if you could reach and
touch the sky. Summer evenings were warm and gentle,
the sun slowly sinking below the skyline, staining the
sky with a pinky glow. It was springtime when he died
and the flowers in the forest were starting to bloom. The
birds were chirping happily in the trees and you tried to

.ax as you left the path and strode through the tangled undergrowth and into the clearing were you had built a small wooden bench to sit on together. The wind hit you, a gentle breeze, as you sat down but the bench seemed too empty without him to squeeze beside you so you sat on the damp grass and watched the lapping waves hit the cliff below. Your hair drifted off your shoulders and an invisible wave washed over you and for one minute you were relieved from the sadness and anger that inside was eating through you. You knew what you had to do.

You went back to the house and after checking on Mother, you went upstairs and walked slowly down the corridor. Past your bedroom and your mother's new room, as she could not bear to sleep in the same room where you could smell his strong aftershave, and where his clothes still hung patiently in the wardrobe, waiting to be worn. Past the bathroom and the study, where together you had discovered the world through pictures and story books. You stopped at the last door and slowly turned the dusty doorknob. A cold, silent draught hit you as you entered. You felt a tear form in your eye but you wiped it away before it had escaped. You walked over to his bedside table and wiped your fingers over the dusty surface. You opened the drawer and took out a single scrapbook, the cover worn from years of handling. You wiped the dust off the front, handling it as if it would save your life, and sitting down on the bed, neatly laid, waiting for his return, you opened the pages and looked over the pictures of you together, fulfilling your dreams, on top of a mountain in Switzerland, skiing in France, rock climbing in Italy. You had promised each other to never give up hope and you didn't want to break your last promise to him.

He had promised you would see it all and that is exactly what you were going to do, with or without him being beside you. He was still in your heart and you knew he would still be with you every step you made, every border you crossed, every country you visited.

He had died and you had died inside, but he still lived on in you and he wanted you to live a happy life with the past that you had together and the future you will have as one.

Abigail McDougall
Tunbridge Wells Girls' Grammar School

TWENTY-ONE

'Not again Jonathan!' exclaimed Bethany Willis, the wife of Jonathan Willis for over twenty years, throwing a newspaper that sat on her lap onto the floor.

'Beth, it's just a camera, it doesn't mean anything. What's wrong with you?' Jonathan said cheekily.

'What's wrong with me? You're the one who lost the camera, then lied to me about losing it!' Beth said, hurt.

'OK, I'm sorry honey; I tried to tell you, I just – jus-'

'Lied?' interrupted Beth fiercely. 'I wouldn't mind if it was just once or twice but you do it on a daily basis! And it's seriously affecting OUR relationship. Jon, I can't keep living like this.'

'What?' Jonathan's eyes started to water.

'You're sleeping on the couch tonight,' Beth said weakly, ignoring her husband's question, trying to hold back tears, and running upstairs.

In the house, there was a sudden ear-splitting silence that Jonathan couldn't take. He lay there on the couch rummaging through his thoughts.

Why do I keep doing this? I need to sort this out

*before I further endanger my relationship. I can't help it; it's just how I react. I am a compulsive liar. I do love Bethany more than anything in the world and if I lost her ... I wouldn't be able to live with myself. From now on I'm going to be completely honest with her. **I promise.***

Whilst Jonathan was reflecting deeply on his actions, Bethany was thinking of a cunning plan to prevent Jonathan from lying. Then she had a wicked idea.

I need to test Jonathan. I want to see if he will be honest with me. I need to take something big, something important ... I know – his wedding ring! He always takes it off at night and leaves it on our bedside table, that would be the perfect opportunity to see if Jonathan tells me or not.

Satisfied, Bethany fell asleep with a smug smile on her face, waiting for the next morning when all would be revealed ...

The next day, Jonathan sincerely apologised to Bethany.

'Beth, you know how bad I feel about all of this. I just hope you can forgive me. *I promise* not to ever lie to you again – even in the most tempting situations.' And they embraced and hugged each other.

'How about we go out to town today, have a relaxing day out in the sun?' Jon suggested.

'Yeah, that would be nice,' Beth said, picking up her sunglasses.

As they were about to leave their house, Beth lied to Jon, saying that she had forgotten something.

'I'll be right back Jon, I think I forgot my phone.'

Beth ran quickly upstairs and started rapidly looking for her husband's ring.

'Where is it?' she yelled agitatedly. 'Ah-ha, found it!'

She snatched it up and secretly put it in the inside pocket of her cardigan to keep it safe.

'Are we ready now?' Jon asked impatiently, waiting by the door.

'Yes sweetie, let's go to town!'

It was a lovely day in the city, with sun, smiles and happiness. Bethany and Jonathan walked hand in hand like a regular middle-aged couple. They visited florists, antique shops and even an old-fashioned traditional French bakery.

'*Merci beaucoup,*' Jonathan said in his best French accent.

'*Amusez-vous bien,*' replied Leonardo the chef (it said written on his label), handing over their pains aux chocolats and croissants.

Over by the road, next to the supermarket, was a field in which they both decided to eat their pastries. Jon gluttonously took a big bite of his pastry and immediately realised his wedding ring was missing from his finger. His heart began racing and his palm became sweaty. Bethany noticed him vary his behaviour and asked if he was OK.

'Yes, honey, I'm fine,' Jonathan said, carefully inspecting Beth's finger.

He stood up and began feeling his pockets to see if the ring had magically fallen there.

'Oh no! What have I done?' Jonathan blurted out.

'What do you mean? Have you lost something?' Beth saw the look of anguish cross his face.

Come on Jon, it's now or never. Are you going to tell Beth the truth, or not?

'No Beth, I haven't lost anything,' Jon said guiltily.

'I guess not,' replied Beth. 'Remember Jon, you can tell me anything. We shouldn't keep secrets from each other, we should be capable of being open to each other about anything.'

Beth stood up and threw the pastry wrapper in the bin.

After that, they continued their walk through the

streets of Brighton.

'Oh look Jon – a wedding ring shop! Let's go and look at some gorgeous rings!'

'But we've already got rings, why do we need to look at some more?' Jon was beginning to become restless. 'It's fine Beth, I'll wait out here until you've finished …'

'No, Jon, I want you to come in and see what type of rings you like,' Beth replied.

'Wait … hang on a second,' Jon said abruptly. 'Why do you want me to look at the rings so much? You know, don't you?'

'Wha – what are you talking about?' Beth gulped nervously.

'The ring! You purposely took my wedding ring in spite – to see my reaction, Bethany, didn't you?' Jonathan asked seriously.

'Fine, you got me. But it was only for the benefit of our relationship …'

'No Beth, you are being a hypocrite,' Jon interrupted. 'You did exactly what you told me not to do. You went behind my back and lied. For a moment there I honestly thought I had lost my ring.'

Jon glared at Beth, who looked upset.

'Bethany, I'm sorry it's just that we both need to reflect on our own behaviour before fixing other's,' Jon said wisely.

'No, I should be apologising,' Beth said responsibly, giving her husband a big hug.

Promising is easy. Living up to the promise is hard.

Xi'ann Minors Dodd
St Catherine's School, Twickenham

TWENTY-TWO

A man rushed into the King's chambers, carrying a small ivory writing set, which he placed on the wooden table. At his master's instruction he withdrew hastily, leaving the King alone. Only this morning he had received the news that his dear family were no longer safe, and now he was desperate to warn them. He had already summoned his most prestigious messenger so he scribbled down the grave news, and had the letter delivered to his messenger, demanding that he should leave 'as soon as the horses are ready'. Within the hour the messenger said his farewells to the King and rode off, a small scroll hidden inside his boot.

On a crumbling stone wall that marked where the safety of his village ended and the danger of the forest began, a small boy, with auburn hair and bright, playful green eyes, was perched. No one entered the forest unless they were hunting, and even that was under duress. There were rumours of purple trolls and minute pixies that would eat your eyes whole lurking in there! The boy contemplated a large bruise on the apple he was eating, deciding that it was disgusting he threw it into the wood, imagining pixies fighting each other for turns to gnaw at it, but soon he grew bored. Suddenly he heard a horse whinnying beyond the wall, but no one ever rode through the forest! Then he heard a shout, full of pain and anger. Something is happening in there, he thought. Whether it was curiosity or a desire to help, he found himself sprinting through the bracken, ducking trees and listening for desperate whinnies that would guide him to his goal. He ran into small clearing and found himself staring at an injured man, spread-eagled, his eyes half closed. Blood trickled from a gaping wound, staining the ground around him. The boy put an arm around the man, in the vain hope of helping him up, but he let out a shout of pain and opened his eyes. His fading eyes searched his surroundings and then fell upon the boy before him.

'What's yo...your n...n...name boy?' the man wheezed.

'Um, Jon Brooks, sir. Don't talk, I'll call for –'

'There's no time, I'm dying. Listen, I need you do something for me boy, it will take great courage but the King will be forever in your debt. Will you do it?'

Jon nodded hesitantly.

'I'm going to send you on a real adventure,' he mumbled and then he instructed Jon to remove a thin scroll from his boot. He continued, 'Go north until you reach Inverness and go to the castle. You must give them this,' he held out the scroll for him to take but Jon paused.

'I'm sorry sir, I don't think I'm the right person for this job, I'm just the baker's son. I'll fetch someone –'

'No you can't! The family are in danger. You must hurry, before it's too late. Please. Take my horse and my sword – I don't need them any more.'

'Please, sir. I'll take you to the doctor and then you

can keep on going!' but the man smiled, a regretful smile, 'No lad; I've lost too much already. Go. Now.'

Jon had been riding, unsuccessfully, for an hour. Having never ridden before and on a horse that was too large for his short legs to reach comfortably, he was continually bumped about on the saddle like a broken jack-in-the-box. The horse's insistence on cantering made his surroundings a blur. Eventually Jon was forced to stop because of an agonising pain in his lower back and the realisation he was very lost; the man had given him a strange circular device, telling him to go in the direction of the arrows' point, but he didn't trust it. He was lost, hungry and exhausted. But the man's words were still ringing in his ears; he knew he was someone's last hope! He struggled back onto the horse and continued through the pouring rain. After many hours he came to a small village where he nearly collapsed in relief. He found the inn, and ate a hearty meal in the corner of a dimly lit room next to the door. Suddenly, seven armed men entered; he heard their drunken banter, and later, their talk of upcoming business. His insides turned into a withering snake as he overheard their murderous plans. Abruptly he stood up and left the inn, determined to reach the castle before these men. He rode on, fighting to stay awake, and comforted himself with the thought that the men did not know who he was. However, despite his best attempts, his mind kept returning to the vast swords and axes at their belts.

Fear, adrenalin and cold kept him awake that night. He rode on, asking directions from several traders, finally sighting the outline of Inverness castle on the horizon. This gave him a surge of confidence, so he dug his heels in, urging the horse to move faster. His heart was pounding as he dismounted and ran up the elegant stone steps, surrounded by a beautiful garden, but he noticed none of this, so determined was he deliver the letter. He knocked repeatedly on the oak door, until it was opened by a servant who quickly led him through to a small room.

'So,' said a voice, making him jump, 'why is my brother sending a boy to do a man's job?'

Jon rapidly explained to the young woman about finding the dying messenger, his subsequent adventure, and finished by passing her the now crinkled and ripped scroll.

As she read her face grew as pale as a corpse. When she had finished she simply turned to the servant and said, 'We need to go now. You know what to do.'

The sound of breaking glass reached them, and everyone fell silent.

Bethany Hayes
Streatham and Clapham High School

TWENTY-THREE

'Taylor, promise me you won't tell anyone. If my parents find out, they'll freak,' pleaded Faye.

'I promise.' I sighed and walked away, leaving her alone in the deserted alleyway.

'I can't believe you're going home in a week,' Faye sighs.

'I know,' I reply. I love London, where I live, but nowhere is quite like New York with its towering skyscrapers, yellow cabs and non-stop buzz. Faye changes the channel on the TV and freezes, the colour draining from her face. I look at the TV. I recognise the street where I left Faye yesterday to meet her 'friend'. 'A body has been found in the Meatpacking District under the High Line,' the reporter is saying. 'A man named Peter Davis. He died from severe head injuries, possibly from banging his head on the kerb.'

The image on the screen changes to show a man who looks like he is in his mid-twenties. I look at Faye, whose face hasn't yet returned to its normal colour, and I remember how when she came back yesterday her eyes were swollen, as if she had been crying. I remember how she checked if I had told anyone where she'd been, even though she knows I always keep my promises. She isn't involved in this, is she?

'Let's go out,' Faye suggests abruptly, turning off the TV.

'Okay,' I say, wondering why Faye is so eager to get out all of a sudden. I grab my black denim jacket and my new leather bag. We step outside the house and walk down the quiet streets of Greenwich Village in a comfortable silence which, of course, I am the first to break by saying something stupid.

'So what happened yesterday? Was he nice?' I don't bother to sound supportive; she knows what I think of her meeting people that she's only ever talked to online.

'Yeah. We went to Starbucks. He was more into me than I was into him,' she mumbles, unable to meet my eyes. I can tell this isn't the truth. Why would she lie to me?

'So, what should we do today?' I ask, trying to change the subject. 'I still haven't been to loads of shops here.'

Faye grins. Shopping always cheers her up.

Hours later, after we have spent all our money in Urban Outfitters and the Converse shop, we sit in Max Brenner's, a chocolate shop near The Strand, and I treat myself to a chocolate syringe whilst she toys with an Oreo milkshake.

'Is something wrong?' I ask. I know I shouldn't push her to tell me, but I can't help it. 'When the TV showed the man who died, you looked like you recognised him. And I know you weren't telling me the truth about the guy you met yesterday. Did you ...' I trail off but she knows what I was going to say. The unspoken words hang in the air.

'Have anything to do with it?' she finishes for me

after a while, a bitter tone in her voice. 'You're supposed to be my friend, Taylor.'

Suddenly, she bursts into tears. I'm not quite sure what to do. Does she want me to comfort her after what I just said? Luckily, the tears stop as quickly as they started.

'I'm sorry,' she sniffs.

'It's okay. Let's go back to your house,' I say, and signal to the waiter for the bill.

A while later, we are admiring ourselves in the large mirror in Faye's bedroom, trying on our new clothes. Faye sits down on the edge of her bed and inspects her nails, something she always does when she is nervous. I sit beside her and wait for her to say something.

'I might have killed that man yesterday. I pushed him because he started attacking me and I was defending myself and he fell and banged his head on the kerb really hard but I checked his pulse and he was still breathing so I didn't think I killed him, but I mean I still hurt him and I freaked and ran,' she blurts out and then burst into tears.

For a while I sit in a stunned silence, wondering what I should say.

'Listen Faye,' I begin, using the most gentle tone possible, 'you probably didn't kill him if he was still breathing when you left.'

'Well then, who did kill him?' Faye sobs. I don't answer. Faye is right – who else would have killed him?

'How can I live with myself if I killed him?' Faye cries. 'He may have been a creep, but he had family and friends that are probably all mourning his loss right now. He had a life, Taylor, a life that I ended!'

'Faye, you might not have killed him – and if you did, it was just self-defence.' I try to comfort her.

'I probably did kill him. And when the police find out, I'll be spending the rest of my life in an orange jumpsuit,' Faye wails hysterically.

'The police aren't going to find out,' I say reassuringly. Even as I say this, I feel a twinge of doubt. What if there is a shop nearby with a security camera outside? What if someone saw? Maybe telling the police is the right thing for me to do?

'We don't know that,' Faye says – she has finally stopped weeping.

'I won't tell them – I promise,' I tell her. Protecting Faye is the right thing to do – isn't it?

Lucha Partington Momber
Impington Village College
Cambridge

TWENTY-FOUR

Reaching for her hand, I stared into her beautiful eyes. I was so close, so close to her. Warmth filled my heart, she was here and we were together, just like we'd promised. Suddenly, I was wrenched away from her by an invisible force. Pain hit me, and I could barely stop myself from screaming. I was thrown into the air, as the ground beneath me seemed to crumble. Everything was breaking and erupting, but she was still there, calling my name. I felt myself falling, falling into nothingness. Black showered over my vision.

Sitting up, I felt sweat trickle down my forehead as I stared around. Nothing had changed; I was still in this hell hole. I noticed the empty bed rolls from yesterday's raid and I realised that could so easily have been me. Rolling over, I readied myself for today's work. Fear slithered through me; I still hadn't adjusted to the trenches. Looking around, I felt my skin crawl. Dirt and grime was everywhere, covering us, we were never clean. Then there were the rats. They scurried in and out, filling the night air with their squeaking, disturbing our sleep; there was no escape from them or the lice. Pushing myself out of bed, I embarked on the futile task of attempting to dislodge some of the dirt. Despite the fear I was ready, ready to fight, ready to risk my life and ready to survive for her. She was the reason I was here, I had decided to join the army to make a better life for her. With every waking moment I missed her. I missed her beautiful eyes, the way she smiled and laughed, and most of all I missed her voice. Suddenly a beefy hand hit my shoulder, and the gruff voice seemed to deafen me. 'You ready for today? Because we are sending you out.' I stared up at his face, his moustache seemed to bristle. I was shocked; this would be my first time. 'Well?' he seemed to yell. I gave a brief nod as he lumbered over to someone else.

Standing in line, I was going out to No Man's Land. The place where barely anyone made it back, where thousands of lifeless corpses rotted. I could feel myself start to panic, as I felt the familiar sensation of terror engulfing me. I heard the officer shout, and I was running as fast as I could but it felt as though I was moving in slow motion. Running towards the barbed fence, I saw my fellow soldiers fall to ground. Blood was everywhere, bodies littered the ground and I felt myself stop. There were bodies everywhere that had once been like me, alive. I shook myself, I had to keep going, it was the only way. Sprinting as fast as I could, I began to feel hope, I could do this. Without warning, I felt myself thrown backwards and the ground erupt. It was just like my dream, except without her, I was going to die without her. Then the pain hit me, it was agonising, everything felt like it was on fire and it was as though I was being stabbed repeatedly. I could barely breathe and I knew this was the end, but I whispered her name one last time. 'Anne.'

Sitting up with a start, I stared around in shock and

confusion. How did I get here? Out of the corner of my eye, I noticed someone and happiness swept through me. Rolling over I stared at her. Anne was curled up in the chair; fast asleep with her hair flopped over her face. She was so beautiful even asleep. I watched as she stirred, and then she opened her eyes which quickly found mine.

'Hey there stranger,' she said. Sensing my confusion she said, 'You still don't remember do you? The bomb blast that hit you?' She faltered as she saw the grin spread across my face, none of it mattered any more. I was home, home with her.

Our life together began again as we found a new rhythm to our days. Our love was rekindled as we revisited the places together that had started our love. Our eyes were blind to the damage that the war had wreaked on our country; it was like we were transported back in time, to when we first met and where the unbreakable bond that had brought us back together had first developed. My leg was slowly healing from the bomb, and I was walking farther each day, usually with Anne but occasionally on my own. On one of the rare unaccompanied walks, I stopped by Anne's studio to see how her paintings had developed in my absence. The studio was dusty, unused and I noticed letters spilling out over the mat, addressed to me. I opened a couple and confusion filled me, what loss were they sorry for? Who had died? I felt Anne's presence at the door and turned to see her face flushed with anger. She marched over to me and tried to rip the letters out of my hand.

'You weren't supposed to see those,' her voice said accusingly. 'We promised, remember?' I stared at her, just stared and then I noticed it. Something was wrong with her eyes; they seemed to be completely black. I felt myself gasp. 'It's you, you're dead.' Her mouth curved into a soundless scream as she shattered into a million pieces.

Looking all around me I felt as if my heart was shattering, she was gone. I felt a tear trickle down my face, I couldn't take it. Suddenly I noticed a flash of movement. Turning around, I came face to face with Anne. Shock ran through me, and then I noticed what she was holding, a knife covered in blood. Only then did I feel the pain pour through me and as the darkness rolled in I heard Anne's voice whisper, 'We promised, together forever.'

Lorna Mead
Gateways School, Leeds

TWENTY-FIVE

'It's going to be all right.' That was the promise I made to my younger brother, I remember it so clearly. I was in an abandoned basement with my brother. We were low on supplies so I went to look around and while I was looking around, something just caught the corner of my eye, something that glinted like gold. I went to the strange metallic object and found out that it was a coin, but it wasn't a coin I knew about. It was old but well-polished and the writing on it wasn't familiar.

As I went to pick up the coin, I had a vision, a vision of my death. It was so vivid I actually thought I had died then and there. The only thing to stop me from collapsing was my brother. He asked if everything was fine, with real sincerity in his voice. I feared for his health and so all I replied with was, 'It's going to be all right.' I didn't know what weight the words would carry. They could strengthen our bond or shatter it.

My memory was empty of that day except for my dream. All I dreamt of was that vision, it was replaying over and over in my head, and I was reliving my own personal hell. As I slowly rose back to conscious, something felt odd, something was missing. This feeling finally was answered when I tried standing up and immediately slumped back down to the floor. Somehow, I had lost the use of my right arm. The panic was rising inside me. Confusion with panic made me think of my brother, there all alone in this world with my body slumped next to him. That thought gave me courage. I had to survive for my brother

As I slumped back down from my failed standing, my brother woke. My brother's curiosity took a hold of him. 'What was that thump?' With this, I simply replied with, 'One of our bags must have fallen off the shelf.' He believed me.

It took all my willpower to carry on through the day as normal as possible so my brother wouldn't suspect anything was wrong. If my brother suspected something, it would cause a stroke if he knew what it was. His doctor told him, 'A stroke of any kind in your current condition would surely kill you.' Because of this, I've dedicated my life to protecting my brother ever since the country began to crumble. We've held through hard times and this wasn't going to stop me.

The day went by, hour by hour, with nothing out of the usual happening. We ate and we slept. But my dream wasn't normal, it was different to my previous dream. This dream, reality wasn't there, nothing. It was like my death scene but I was already dead; it was like I had truly died.

I had a rude awakening by a sharp stab of pain; the pain was coursing through my arm like it was trying to kill me from the inside. The pain was unbearable and so was my shout. Any sound would wake my brother but a shout, who knew what would happen. Luckily, my brother simply woke without anything problematic happening.

'What was that?' With a hint of fear in his voice. I responded like I did the first time, 'It's going to be all right.'

I had to tell my brother that both my arms weren't working. He would definitely have a stroke if he knew I kept it hidden but I can't rely on my brother like this. He needs me and if I'm useless, what's the point of living. All these thoughts seemed stupid when I thought about my brother. All alone with me slumped by his side. 'No' I thought. I must be tough, for him.

I explained to my brother about my disability. He kept asking questions about my health and whether I was in danger. It took all my willpower from pouring out all over him. I kept lying, saying everything was fine and generally trying to ease his panic. My brother didn't know but I did; I was not long for this world. Holding that information from my brother was eating me up. I didn't know if I should just make it easy for myself. The thought of my brother was what gives me strength that is why what I must stop.

This dream was the worst of all. My teeth clenched as I was falling asleep, I did not want to dream but I had no control. This dream, it was about my brother. My arms were fine and so were my legs but, my brother; he didn't have the use of his arms or his right leg. It tore me in two to see him like this. All broken and useless, I could even hear him saying, 'Kill me.' These few words are what struck a hole through my heart. A hole that can't be healed. All I said, no, whispered, 'It's going to be all right.'

I woke to a shriek. I was suddenly up without knowing that it was my own. I seemed to have slept well and my brother was already up preparing some breakfast from the food that we got yesterday. He just stood there in shock at me. I asked him what I said. He said, 'Kill me.' I tried walking up to him but my right leg wasn't functioning. I beckoned him over. When he arrived, I gave him a big hug and I explained to him about my dreams I told him, 'It's going to be all right.'

This promise is everything. This promise was everything. We all live and we die but we are never ready for it. This promise is what allowed me to accept my fate. This promise was my brother. This promise was what was going to kill me.

Ethan Hillman
John Henry Newman Catholic College
Birmingham

TWENTY-SIX

Hide Tabby! This was the motto of her life. If she didn't find a good hiding place, then Steve would find her. Tabitha's sharp ears heard the metallic clicking sound once the car had been parked. With one mighty leap, she squeezed onto the top shelf of the cupboard. It was uncomfortable and smelt musty but she was safe. At least she thought she was. An angry, bellowing lion roar rumbled throughout the whole house, making it shake violently like an earthquake. Steve had found the spill on his brand new jacket. She had tried to lick the stain clean, yet still there was a pale white tint from the stain which was still damp as well slightly sticky. Tabby pushed herself as far back as she could, but she knew it wasn't good enough. Run. That is the only option. Tabby crept out of the cupboard and tentatively walked down the steps. She was concentrating so much on moving swiftly, silently, but speedily that she didn't notice what she had bumped into. Hesitantly, she looked up. Two legs were in front of her. Steve. His face had a plaster of anger, but deep down she knew he was drunk. He always was. Mustering up all her courage, she ran with all her might and scampered out of the lime-green door. Steve ran out and threw a bottle of alcohol at her. The bottle smashed and millions of shards flew everywhere.

She ran into the road. She looked for somewhere to escape, to break free. Right. Left. Up. Down. It was too late. The car was approaching. There was something about this car that was niggling at the back her memory. It somehow looked familiar. Mum? The car stopped at a sudden halt. Mum stormed out of the seven-seater car. The expression on her face was unmistakable – she was angry. However, deep in her eyes, she saw disappointment and sadness. She had always shouted at Tabby but deep down, she thought Mum loved her. But she knew she had done it. Tabby had blown her last chance.

3 years later

'Why do you always listen to him, Mum?' Tabitha shouted, with the burning sensation of tears prickling her eyes. 'All he does is drink – he's no father to me and he will never be. He leaves us for months and when he comes back, saying he's sober, EVERY time you believe he's changed – "Oh just give him one more chance, Tabby!" she said, sarcasm dripping from her voice. 'And now, you're going to listen to him again and cart me off to a care home. How could you? You're no mother to me.' Tabitha climbed out of the black Toyota, with large wet patches on her clothes.

'Wait, Tabby, before you go, I promise I'll come back for you! I promise!' Ruth exclaimed.

'Don't bother! Goodbye Ruth.'

Ruth woke up with a sweaty face and breathing heavily. She glanced at the clock – it was 9 am – she'd overslept.

Clambering out of bed, she knew she had to forget about the dream. But how could she? That was the worst day of her life, the day she sent her girl to a care home. She couldn't afford to be late. Tabitha would never forgive her. This was her one chance to rebuild the relationship with her little girl.

Ruth splashed water on her face. It was time to forget about the devastating past and plan for the bright, happy future ahead. Ruth whispered to herself: 'I am coming for you Tabby!'

The tension around Ruth could be squeezed as easily as a citrus lemon. She was going to see her girl after three years. She drove along the rough, rocky road, with anticipation. Sunlight slashed the clean blackout windows of the car. After a long drive, still wandering in her thoughts, Ruth arrived at Evergreen Home.

The Home had changed, for the worse. It seemed derelict, abandoned. Murky-green moss and dandelions were carpeting the pathway, growing in between paving slabs. On the sides of the pathway, noxious weeds were widening. Towering oak trees were swaying in the harsh wind, the yellow warmth of the autumn sun was still peeping through the almost-gone leaves. The horrible sound of a solitary, screeching eagle snapped her back to reality from the appalling appearance of the Home. Gingerly, she walked along the rotten pathway and knocked on the bulky wooden door. A muscular man opened the door and looked down at her, disgusted. Ruth stared at him with dread.

'Who are you?' he asked in a deep, gruff voice.

'My name is Ruth Cosby. I'm here to see my girl – Tabitha Cosby. I have all the letters of confirmation right here,' she said rummaging through her handbag, trying to find the letters. Once she found the crumpled papers, she showed them to him. She looked at the man's badge. It read:

Nathan Green
Staff
Evergreen House
Head Care Worker

Nathan chuckled. It was a deep, hollow laugh that made her insides curl up.

'Tabitha's just around the corner,' he said while opening a rusty, creaky gate.

He led her behind the large house. Amongst many homes, one had 'Tabitha' written on it with a navy blue marker pen. Tabby, recognising a familiar smell, leapt out of her home and nudged against Ruth, affectionately. Ruth smiled and picked up Tabby, staring into her greenish-yellow eyes. She knew that Tabby still missed her.

Because cats, they never forget. And sometimes, promises are broken so they can be fixed.

Madhura Sivakumar
Lancaster Girl's Grammar School

TWENTY-SEVEN

We were six. We were lying in our fort that protected us from all evil. The rain was lashing down outside, it was like a load of rocks were falling onto the roof. I shone a torch at Daniel.

'I need to tell you a secret,' I said.

He looked at me intently.

'Do you promise not to tell anyone?'

He locked his crystal blue eyes with mine: 'I promise.'

'Promise, promise, promise?'

'I promise. Tell me Sylvie.'

I took a deep breath.

'I ... I saw my daddy kill someone,' I whispered. Daniel went as white as a ghost and his mouth dropped open. There was silence.

'I saw him holding a knife and push someone against a wall and then ... then the body fell. I've never told anyone about it and I've never asked him about it.'

Daniel didn't say anything. He didn't even blink. Finally ...

'Umm … do you know who the body was?'

'No. I got scared and ran. Do you promise not to tell?'

Daniel looked concerned. 'I promise.' He held out his hand. I locked my fingers around his. 'I'll never tell.'

We were sitting on a table outside our favourite café, the sun was shining down on us as if it was smiling. Daniel was telling me about this party that he was invited to. It sounded really cool but I wasn't invited.

'Sylvie?'

'Yeah?'

'Do you want to come with me? Alex will be fine with it.'

'Umm, no thanks. I'm not much of a partier. But thanks anyway.'

'What do you mean you're not much of a partier? You went to a party last weekend!'

'Oh yeah. Well, I guess I'm all partied out then.'

'Sylvia. What's going on? You're always up for a party. Is it something about your dad?'

I looked down at my steaming coffee and took a sip. It burnt my tongue. He looked at me with a concerned face as I licked the froth from around my mouth.

'Sylvie. Spill.'

I sighed. 'I've blanked out most of what happened when I was younger but parts of it remain in my mind. They appear in my dreams, haunting me. I want to get rid of them but I can't.'

'What do you remember?'

'I remember crouching down behind a bin, it was dark. I remember two silhouettes, an angry voice which was my dad and a crying voice, it was a woman's voice and I … I can't remember anything else.'

Daniel dropped some coins. They rolled round in circles until they clattered to the ground. It triggered something in my mind. A vision.

'I remember!' I exclaimed. 'The lady was holding coins in her hand. She was going to give him money but then he killed her. The coins dropped from her hand as she collapsed to the ground. The coins fell just like yours did. Also, my mum knows about it. I heard them talking about it.'

'I'm so sorry Sylvie.'

He came over to me and gave me a hug. He still gave hugs like he did when he was six. I breathed in. He still smelt like he did when he was six. He smelt of coconuts and posh fragrances. His mum had posh fragrances in every room of the house. It felt so welcoming.

'Maybe I could live with you,' I said with a cheeky grin.

As he laughed, his signature dimples appeared. 'I don't really think I want to see you more than I already do.'

'Hey!' I laughed as I threw a piece of muffin at him.

We were silent for a couple of minutes as the birds sang their songs and the busy ladies darted in and out of shops like ping pong balls.

Daniel cleared his throat. 'What about this party then?'

'Umm, I guess it would keep my mind off things.'

'That's a yes then!' His face lit up with excitement. He slurped down the rest of his coffee and stood up.

'I'll pick you up at seven,' he said as he ruffled my knotty, black hair. 'Dress for dancing!' He shouted down the high street.

I finished my coffee and stuffed the rest of my muffin in my coat pocket. I stood up and strolled home down the summery high street.

I looked at the time, 6:45. I had my dress on and my earrings were in place. My dress was just above my knees and a midnight blue colour. It was a sea of silk. I sprayed my favourite perfume and headed downstairs to wait. Suddenly Daniel burst in through the door.

'Hello!' he said cheerily.

I walked out of the cosy sitting room and went to meet him.

'Oh my god!' he gasped.

Hoping he would say I looked amazing, I breathed in.

'You look disgusting!' he blurted.

'Wow. What a good friend you are, giving me that self-esteem boost.'

'Only joking Sylvie! You look lovely. Come one let's go.'

We got to the town hall (where the party was) and there were people piling in from every direction. When we got in you could barely move! We were all squashed together like teeth in a mouth. It was incredibly hot and the air was all clammy. There was a massive disco ball hanging from the ceiling and there were colourful lights bouncing off the walls.

I started to talk to some people and I felt better. We then went and danced and it was really fun. After wondering where Daniel was, I saw he had suddenly appeared on stage – a little tipsy!

'I'd like to say something,' he shouted. The music stopped and everyone looked at him.

'Sylvia's dad …'

Oh no … My face went red and I started to feel sick. Don't say it.

Louisa Boden
The King's School in Macclesfield

TWENTY-EIGHT

I must've played the Bach Adagio a hundred times
before – it was his favourite – but today was different.
Today my hands were trembling as I picked up my bow.
I grasped the neck of my cello with my tiny, bony hand
and held it close. Fumbling, I plucked at the strings with
stiffened fingers to check they were in tune. My heart
was pounding inside my chest as the notes echoed round
the room. Beads of sweat broke out across my forehead.
As the cold night air drifted in through the open door,
you could almost smell my fear.

'Get on with it!' the commandant bellowed. 'Play,
boy, play!'

With bowed head, I felt his dark presence before me.
There in the lamplight he stood, in his shiny, blackened
boots and tightly pressed uniform – the swirling swastika
emblazoned on his arm.

I closed my eyes tight, to shut him out. I had to calm
my nerves. I tried hard to remember my little music
room at home, all those months ago. But that was before
– it felt like another lifetime. What was it the maestro

had taught me back in Vienna? I drew a deep breath from somewhere inside of me and began to play. As soon as the music flowed though me I could feel his anger subsiding. A strange silence fell over the camp as it did most nights – a silence broken only by the sound of my notes. The piece had a haunting, fragile beauty that had no place there.

The commandant listened intently, as he always did, standing in the doorway and staring out at the rows of wooden huts huddled together in the darkness. This had become our common ritual – just me and the commandant. He was a menacing, brutal man who ordered senseless killing by day, but by night he lost himself in the music. It seemed to cast a special sort of magic over him. Perhaps he found comfort in the mellow tones of my playing. I didn't really care. In fact, I hated him with every fibre of my being, but it was his passion for my playing that kept me alive. As long as I brought him Bach every evening, I was one of the lucky ones. I was spared.

Perhaps that is why I was so terrified when the others asked me to send the message. A shift in key was all it would take, they said. 'D minor' for danger and a switch to a major key when the coast was clear. They had it all worked out. Communication between the prisoners was almost impossible, but from my privileged position I could get the message across. I could see whereabouts the guards were on their patrol. And so it was that tonight my music was woven into their plan. The Adagio was to become a weapon and a warning system.

They'd been digging the tunnel for weeks and now they were ready to make a run for it – desperate to get out. Under cover of darkness, they planned to break free of the perimeter fence and escape while the commandant was distracted. But the timing was everything. Only a few seconds separated the guards' patrol and the deadly glare of the searchlights. It all depended on me and my music. As I played, the sweet melody of the minor bars sang through the night. I thought of all those souls who had gone before me, of the long grey lines of shaven heads and shrunken shoulders, boys hunched like old men as they shuffled out of the trucks.

My head was hurting as I came to the crescendo, but still I played on like one possessed. My mouth was dry, my eyes were fixed as I stared beyond the commandant into the darkness outside. My fear was unnoticed as he lost himself in the music.

Seconds later, I heard the crunching of gravel underfoot. The guards marched past and I saw my moment. Time for the message. Quickly, I changed key.

My fingers began to climb the major scales. The notes lifted high into the air and pierced the silence. As I slid through the melody I prayed the commandant would not notice my sudden shift. He turned slowly and looked at me. Still I played on. Faster and faster. Louder and louder like the deathly cries I had heard so many times coming from deep inside the chamber at the other end of the camp.

He took a step towards me and our eyes met. A flash of recognition sped across his face and in that instant he knew. He lunged at me in fury and let out a yell. It was strange, like a wounded animal. But it came too late. The message had been delivered. The others had escaped. Even as my cello lay in pieces on the floor beside me, and a sticky trickle of blood seeped slowly from my head, I knew in my heart I had won.

The commandant crushed my fingers under his boot with no more effort than it took to kill a fly. But there was music in my head as the pain shot through me. I smiled weakly and thought I could hear their hurried footsteps in the darkness. I felt sure they had got through the perimeter fence. My body was light. I could not move. As my mind began to drift there was a shift in key and I could see them fleeing to the safety and cover of the woods beyond.

Felix Ross
New College School, Oxford

TWENTY-NINE

Sam Andrews sat in his bed, wide awake, listening to the sounds of the night. His house smelt old and musty and the bed sheets were as hard as a brick. He heard a creak from the floorboards outside his bedroom. The door swung wide open.

Sam shrieked as his cat Tim crept in. 'Oh Tim,' Sam gasped, 'I am so glad you're here, I was getting so creeped out.'

'Meow.'

'(Yawn) I love you Tim.' With that, Sam fell asleep.

The next morning when Sam came down for breakfast Tim wasn't in the garden playing with the pigeons as he usually was. 'Where is he?' he thought to himself. Sam went into the kitchen. 'Mum, Dad, it's time for breakfast.'

'Where are they?' Sam thought. 'I am sure they came home from the party last night, at least I hope they did.' As Sam ate he was thinking about everything that could have happened to his parents. 'I must stop thinking about this, maybe a little TV will empty my head.'

Sam finished his breakfast and sat in front of the TV. 'Ah this is the life, the TV and me, how I love it,' Sam thought. 'All I need is my cat. Wait a minute … my cat!' Sam turned the house upside down and back to front but there was still no sign of Tim.

As Sam turned round, he noticed the painting on the living room wall. It was a portrait of their old house. Mum loved it because her best friend had painted it. He stepped closer, his heart was pounding and his face was sweating so much that it could be mistaken for a waterfall.

Sam picked up the painting and in the living room window was his mum, his dad and his cat Tim. He gasped. 'How did they get in there?' he asked himself. 'Maybe they were just painted in when they were in that house,' he thought. 'But we only got Tim when we moved to this house so how did he get in there?'

He sat in the living room and thought for about three minutes but still he couldn't come up with a solution. Sam touched the painting, it was dry, how was that possible?

When Sam went to bed that night he felt very lonely, he knew it wouldn't be long before, whatever it was, took him into the painting too.

The next morning, when Sam woke up, he saw that the kitchen had been ransacked, even though it was never tidy before. The cupboards were wide open, the fridge was knocked over and all of the walls were ripped to shreds. He got himself a drink of water and went into the living room. That had been ransacked too. Eventually he came to realise that every room was broken and battered.

The strange thing was that the painting was left intact and so was everything within about one metre of it. 'How weird,' Sam stuttered. 'It's like the painting has mystical properties.'

If only Sam had noticed the dark shadow behind him maybe his life would have been a whole lot better.

Sam felt a hand on his back. He dare not turn round in fear of whatever it was. He shut his eyes as the hand pushed him into the painting.

When Sam opened his eyes he realised that he was not in his own house but in the garden of his old house. He rubbed his eyes as if he were dreaming. 'I'm in the painting!'

'Meow.'

'Tim,' Sam called with tears of joy; he felt warm fur brush his skin. 'Ah Tim, you don't know how glad I am to see you again.'

Overjoyed, Sam picked Tim up and ran into the house. When he got there he noticed that the paint was starting to fade and run. It was like someone had sprayed it with water. 'My water!' he thought. 'It must have made the painting damp.'

He remembered what his mum had said. 'Be careful Sam, if you get any water on that painting it will run and that will be very bad as it is an irreplaceable piece of artwork.'

'So that is why the painting is running,' he thought, as he realised that he needed to find his parents and get out of there, and fast.

He rushed into the woods at the back of the garden screaming as sharp, pointy prickles tore at his skin. 'Mum, Dad!' Yet he could hear nothing. He rushed back to the house, they were gone. He came to realize that if he and Tim could walk around in the painting so could they.

He ran up the stairs and stood in the doorway of his parents' room. He gasped. Now, where the painting used to be, there was a portal out of the painting. He was about to jump in when he remembered his parents were still lost in the painting. As he turned away he saw the digital wall clock, it seemed to be counting down from one minute, it had already gone past fifty seconds and it wasn't stopping. He realised that it was the countdown for the portal. He looked back at the swirling mass of incredibly bright white light. It was fading slowly, getting smaller and smaller, darker and darker. He knew that he could either save his parents or just himself. Tearing his hair out Sam screeched, 'What should I do?'

The clock reached zero. The portal shut, Sam and Tim were trapped in the painting forever. Meanwhile his parents walked into the living room outside the painting. When they saw the mess on the floor, Sam's dad exclaimed, 'What a shame.'

'I know,' replied his mother. 'I liked that painting.'

Kai Bass
Rydon Community College
West Sussex

THIRTY

I always adored staying with my grandmother. She had a cottage nestled in some woodland. I always imagined it as a magical paradise with the surrounding trees whispering their secrets. Of course it was nothing of the sort and yet it did have its own magic.

Grandfather had long since died. That was always a sadness for me and yet I felt I knew him so well. As for Grandmother, he had never left; she shared so many memories and stories of their life together. For most it would be a place of mourning and yet somehow for Grandma and me it was a place of happiness, peace and contentment. Grandfather was never far away.

Every morning in the spring seemed beautiful, but one particular morning it was even more stunning. Grandmother and I decided to go for a walk around the lake. Along the uneven path, we came across an alluring tree. It had pink and white blossom, which was spread out over all the branches. It towered over us like a fragrant wave. As the wind blew, it started waving at us; I felt as though it was welcoming me back to its woods.

It was Grandmother's favourite type of tree – it was an apple blossom. She always said she had a unique connection with apple blossom because they repeatedly reminded her of Grandfather. I imagined them standing together beneath its boughs, holding hands and talking of the future. The spring is such a season of hope of what's to come. All around you are the signs of promised new beginnings: fledging chicks, prancing lambs and jubilant daffodils. It seemed only fitting that it was beneath this very tree in the spring, just like the day I stood there with Grandmother, that he had proposed.

Grandmother had told me all about it. She was easily transported back to that moment in time. He had knelt on one knee in the formal way but had such a smile on his face as only a sweetheart does, and asked simply, 'Will you be mine forever as my wife?' She told me she had cried. She had tears in her eyes as she told me. 'I was in a trance,' she explained. He had already spoken to her father the previous day and been granted permission. He had needed a little convincing as Grandmother was only eighteen and to him still seemed his little girl. But Grandfather had convinced him of his good intentions and promised to always care of her. He never stopped caring.

I could see the ring on my Grandmother's hand that he had given her. It was a Ceylon sapphire; just beautiful. You could also see around her neck on a simple chain, his wedding ring. I never saw her without either. It seemed that even in death they were inseparable.

Apple blossom was the symbol of my Grandfather's personal promise to my grandmother. He promised that he would stay with her always, which is probably another reason for her consistently talking about him. They both spoke the language of flowers and their meaning, so they both knew that apple blossom was in fact symbolic of promise.

In Grandmother's house there was this beautiful painting that my Grandfather had done. She had told me that it was very special to her and I could see why, because it was also an apple blossom tree, the very one under which Grandfather had proposed. He had given it to her as a wedding gift, so she clearly treasured it, just as much now as when he had first given it to her.

Then it happened. I was with her at the end. She looked so peaceful laying in her bed. She knew she would see him again soon. The doctors said they could do no more for her. If she had been to the clinic earlier perhaps they could have done more for her but I think she knew and didn't want people to worry about her or make a fuss. She was ready. I couldn't imagine life without her. She had taught me so much; not least the language of flowers: yellow rose for friendship, primrose meaning, 'I can't live without you', but it was the apple blossom of promise that always touched me most.

Following the funeral, I went to the cottage. The silence there was painful. I wanted to hear her calling from the kitchen, offering a cup of tea; but I knew it could not be. She was gone. I sat in her chair and breathed in her favourite perfume that still lingered in the air. In that moment I needed anything that would keep her close. I hugged the velvet cushion as I began to sob. Tears flowed uncontrollably. I couldn't stop. Grief is wretched.

I hadn't noticed time pass. It was late afternoon and the shadows across the room were long and I suddenly felt cold. It was at that moment that my own mother entered. I couldn't imagine the pain she was going through. After all she had now lost both her parents. Then, I realised she was carrying something. She offered it to me. 'She wanted you to have this,' she explained simply. It was my grandfather's painting of the apple blossom. 'She said you would know and understand its value,' she added rather quizzically. I didn't want to explain it then. I would tell my fiancé when I gave it to him. He would have my Promise.

Hannah Richardson
The Holy Trinity C of E Secondary School
Crawley

THE AUTHORS

National Short Story Week Young Writer 2015

Overall winner: Amber Lahdelma, Tunbridge Wells Girls' Grammar School

Year 8 girls
Winner:
Julia Harman, The King's School in Macclesfield
Runners up:
Louisa Boden, The King's School in Macclesfield
Abigail McDougall, Tunbridge Wells Girls' Grammar School

Year 7 girls
Winner:
Amber Lahdelma, Tunbridge Wells Girls' Grammar School
Runners up:
Xi'ann Minors Dodd, St Catherine's School, Twickenham
Georgina Gadian, Streatham and Clapham High School

Year 8 boys
Winner:
Joe Wald, Dulwich Prep London
Runners up:
Kian Taylor, The Holy Trinity C of E Secondary School, Crawley
Danny Matten, The Holy Trinity C of E Secondary School, Crawley

Year 7 boys
Winner:
Sam Cohen, Dulwich Prep London
Runners up:
Ethan Hillman, John Henry Newman
Louis Partridge, Dulwich Prep London

Highly commended
Mia Catton, St Catherine's School, Twickenham
Lorna Mead, Gateways School, Leeds
Lucha Partington Momber, Impington Village College, Cambridge
Isla Patterson, St Catherine's School, Twickenham
Maddison Pick, Gateways School, Leeds
Caitlin Piper, St Catherine's School, Twickenham
Hannah Richardson, The Holy Trinity C of E Secondary School, Crawley
Madhura Sivakumar, Lancaster Girls' Grammar School
Julia Trier, The King's School in Macclesfield

Previous National Short Story Week Young Writer winners and runners up
Kai Bass, Rydon Community College, West Sussex (highly commended for The Choice 2011-2012)
Eleanor Dale, Torquay Girls School (winner, year 7 girls 2011-12 for The Choice)

John James Daley, Dulwich Prep London (highly commended 2012-13 for The Message)

Bethany Hayes, Streatham and Clapham High School (winner, year 8 girls 2012-13 for The Message)

Tom King, Dulwich Prep London (winner 2011-2012 for The Choice)

Ryan Krzyzaniak, St Edmund Arrowsmith, Ashton-in-Makerfield (highly commended for The Choice 2011-2012)

Tara Lewis, New Hall School, Chelmsford (highly commended for The Choice 2011-2012)

Isabelle Owen, St Catherine's School, Twickenham (highly commended 2012-13 for The Message)

Felix Ross, New College School, Oxford (winner 2012-13 for The Message)

TEENAGE CANCER TRUST

All of the royalties from sales of this anthology will go to Teenage Cancer Trust to support them in the work that they do. Here is a message from Teenage Cancer Trust:

Around seven young people between 13 and 24 are diagnosed with cancer every day. Teenage Cancer Trust is the only UK charity dedicated to improving their quality of life and chances of survival. We build specialist units within NHS hospitals bringing young people together to be treated by teenage cancer experts in a place designed just for them.

We also provide specialist staff within our units, including nurses and youth support coordinators. They are experts in teenage and young adult cancer, and provide the best possible clinical care and support.

We want every young person with cancer to have access to this specialist care, no matter where they live.

Traditionally treated alongside children or elderly patients at the end of their lives, young people can feel extremely isolated and scared during treatment, often never meeting another young person with cancer. Being treated alongside others their own age makes a huge difference to their whole experience.

Teenage Cancer Trust believes young people's lives shouldn't stop because they have cancer, and treat them as young people first, cancer patients second. We exist to ensure they have access to the best possible care and professional support from the point of diagnosis.

Providing a place that feels 'normal' and not like an institution helps young people cope with cancer and its gruelling treatments. Our units are designed to feel like a home from home, where young people will be comfortable. The walls are bright, the furniture is funky, there might be a pool table or a jukebox, and there's always a place to watch films and surf the net.

We also educate young people about cancer, providing free cancer awareness sessions to schools, colleges and universities. Cancer in young people is rare but we work to empower young people to take control of their health, learn the common signs of cancer and seek medical advice if they are ever worried.

The five most common signs of cancer in young people are unexplained and persistent:

- Pain (that doesn't go away with pain killers)
- Lump, bump or swelling
- Extreme tiredness
- Significant weight loss
- Changes in a mole

Teenage Cancer Trust provides a range of other services for young people and their families:

Find your Sense of Tumour: an annual weekend bringing 300 young people together to help them understand and deal with the physical and psychological effects of cancer.

Jimmyteens.tv: enables young people to share their cancer experiences creatively through video diaries, films and animation.

www.teenagecancertrust.org: an award winning website and support network for young people with cancer.

International Conference on Teenage and Young Adult Cancer Medicine: the primary event for those working in the field to keep ahead of developments, and to share information and best practice from around the world.

Medical courses – We fund courses for medical professionals at all levels, so they can improve how they treat young people with cancer.

We rely on donations to fund our vital work. You can help transform the lives of young people with cancer. Visit www.teenagecancertrust.org to find out how.

THE GUARDIAN
CHILDREN'S AND TEEN BOOKS

Do you love books?

The Guardian children's and teen books website www.theguardian.com/childrens-books-site is a site written for (and lots of it by) children and teenagers to celebrate books, reading, authors and illustrators.

We welcome new site members under the age of 18 and there are so many ways to get involved. If you go to the site, you'll see a how to join section on the front page which explains exactly how to do it. It's really a matter of emailing us, and it's completely free of charge.

Once you are a member, we send you books to review and also invite our members to interview authors and join in our many discussions (on the site and through social media) and projects on the site.

All our reviews are written by children and teenagers who the books were written for, rather than interested adults – and we think that makes our site full of the best recommendations about.

We are bursting with ideas on what to read next,

competitions and gorgeous galleries, podcasts and videos by authors, and the best in teen writing, and we can't wait to welcome you to the Guardian children's and teen books site!

NATIONAL SHORT STORY WEEK

National Short Story Week is an annual awareness event. The aims of National Short Story Week are to:

1) get more people reading and listening to short stories;
2) get more people writing short stories;
3) develop creative and commercial opportunities for individuals and organisations involved in the short story form.

National Short Story Week is celebrated through events taking place around the UK; in bookshops, libraries, schools, colleges, universities and online. National Short Story Week also features in the national and regional press, on the radio and on a large number of websites and blogs.

For more information about National Short Story Week, including ideas for ways to get involved, go to www.nationalshortstoryweek.org.uk

Printed in Great Britain
by Amazon